Ian

CHRIS KENISTON

USA TODAY BESTSELLING AUTHOR

Indie House Publishing

Indie House Publishing

BOOKS BY CHRIS KENISTON

Aloha Series
Aloha Texas
Almost Paradise
Mai Tai Marriage
Dive Into You
Shell Game
Look of Love
Love by Design
Love Walks In
Waikiki Wedding

Surf's Up Flirts
(Aloha Series Companions)
Shall We Dance
Love on Tap
Head Over Heels
Perfect Match
Just One Kiss
It Had to Be You

Honeymoon Series
Honeymoon for One
Honeymoon for Three

Family Secrets Novels
Champagne Sisterhood
The Homecoming
Hope's Corner

Farraday Country
Adam
Brooks
Connor
Declan
Ethan
Finn
Grace
Hannah
Ian
Jamison

ACKNOWLEDGEMENTS

I've learned a few things recently. The first came as a surprise. As it turns out, writing a book and planning a daughter's wedding is not a good mix for me. Who knew there were so many details to a wedding? Then I discovered it's impossible to spruce up a few things around the house to receive guests without sprucing a lot more. But the nicest thing to come from the chaos of doing too much at once has been the added help from friends.

Without my friends this book would still be in my computer and I'd be pulling out my hair by the roots. Even the ones that aren't gray! Author Dale Mayer knocked down more than one brick wall, helping move the story forward. Both she and my friend Cheryl Lucas practically spoon fed me the end of the story. J.M. Madden, once again saved the day, this time with a chicken bone. Y'all are fantastic!

Ian was a tough story to tell, but I hope y'all get to know him as well as I do and love his story and the Tucker Bluff shenanigans as much as all the other Farradays.

Enjoy!

CHAPTER ONE

There are many things in life which are never a good thing. Death, taxes—and like now—the reflection of flashing red and blue lights in the rear-view mirror.

"I should've stayed at the reception," Kelly Ann Morgan muttered to herself, pulling to the side of the road. "Stupid feet." Despite her mother's warning, she'd opted to wear the sexy slingbacks with five inch heels that made her look tall and something closer to svelte, but even having kicked them off two long hours ago hadn't helped the ache still shooting up her arches. Once Finn and his bride had left the reception, all she could think of was getting off her throbbing feet and crawling into bed. With the others still dancing the night away, she'd convinced the groom's sister to catch a ride with her brother so Kelly could leave on the heels of the newlyweds. If not for her stupid feet she'd still be at the reception dancing with all her friends instead of stopped at the side of the road with a police car on her bumper.

Searching her beaded clutch for her license, she sucked in a calming breath and replayed the last few blocks in her mind, wondering what she could have done wrong. License in hand, she lowered the window and took a quick glance at the windshield. No expired registration. At least that was a good thing.

"Evening, miss. License and proof of insurance please?"

"Yes," *hiccup,* "sir." She stretched out her hand. "I'm sorry." *Hiccup.* "I get hiccups when I'm nervous."

The officer raised his attention from the license to her face. "I see. Wait here, please."

Maybe she had a burned out tail light or something. Staring intently at the rear-view mirror, watching the officer get into the front seat of his patrol car did nothing to ease her unsteady nerves.

He was just checking her insurance. Routine. Standard Operating Procedure. Nothing to be concerned about. After all, she wasn't a criminal on the run.

The towering man sauntered back to her door, his expression unreadable.

Impatient, she blurted out, "Did I do something wrong?"

"There's a stop sign a few blocks back."

"Stop sign?"

His gaze scanned the interior of the car in one swift motion. "Where are you coming from, miss?"

"My friend's wedding." Sucking in a deep breath and swallowing hard, she tried to suppress the stupid nervous hiccups.

"Celebrating?" he asked evenly.

Kelly nodded. She didn't dare open her mouth.

"Have a few drinks?"

"No, sir. Well, yes, sir, but I'm perfectly sober."

The officer nodded and took half a step back. "If you'll step out of the car, please?"

"I had my last drink at least a couple of hours ago." She dangled one foot out the door then another. "Trust me, no one would have let me out the door of the hall if I'd had more." *Hiccup.*

The man's gaze dropped, and for a few exhilarating seconds, she thought he was admiring her legs. "Miss, where are your shoes?"

"Shoes?" Did he mean those miserable expensive torture devices? She flung her thumb over her shoulder in the direction of the backseat only to suddenly realize she had no recollection of tossing them there in the first place. "I… think I forgot them at the reception."

"If you'll please stand with your arms out and raise your right foot six inches off the ground."

"Yes," *hiccup,* "of course, but I can straighten this whole thing out if I could just have a minute to call someone. You see…" Arms spread, she toppled sideways, balancing on one foot had never been her strong suit. She'd flunked out of ballet class at the age of six. Regrouping, she tried again, wobbling precariously before almost tipping over once more. "Oh, forget this. If I could just call—"

The officer raised his flashlight. "Are you refusing the field sobriety test?"

She sucked up her nerve and straightened her shoulders. If standing on one foot was part of the test, she'd never pass it. "I am."

"Then you're definitely going to get your one phone call."

• • • •

"Mom is going to be extremely disappointed the party's almost over and instead of dancing with an eligible female you're dancing with me." Ian Farraday's little sister, Hannah, smiled up at him.

"Only because DJ tapped his future brother-in-law into helping load the wedding gifts." Across the floor he spotted his mother approaching the square patch of dance floor at his father's side. "Besides, if Dad doesn't fade before the song ends, Mom will never notice."

Hannah chuckled. "I guess you and Jamie are lucky she loves dancing more than she loves to sing."

"But Jamie isn't dancing with his sister."

"No." Hannah frowned. "That blonde has monopolized him since Joanna cut the cake."

"You're losing your touch, sis. The blonde was reeling Jamie in before they poured the first glass of champagne."

Hannah's gaze shifted across the big hall to where her eldest brother and the Marilyn Monroe wanna-be twirled to the music. "Jamie had been the one who took best to those dance lessons Mom insisted we all have."

"Helps that he was old enough to understand all the girls love a guy who can take a turn on a dance floor without stepping on their feet." Ian was only a few years younger than his brother, but at the time he'd considered the dance lessons a major imposition on his youthful fun. Not till he was in college and had easily mastered the two step—and winning the best girls—did he realize that once again his mom had been right. Which only made him wonder, briefly, why she'd picked now to harp on his bachelorhood.

The disc jockey announced the last song of the evening and Ian spun his sister to the first notes of the popular tune "Time of Your Life." By the end of the song they were laughing, out of breath, and ready to call it a night.

A few feet from their empty table the sound of a cell phone ringing caught Ian's attention. Quickening his step, he followed the sound, and under the napkin by DJ's seat, uncovered the culprit. The caller ID showed Lew Sterrett Justice Center. Normally he would have let another person's phone go to voice mail, but this late at night, he opted to answer. "Hello."

"DJ?"

"No. DJ will be back shortly. This is Ian. Can I help?"

"I hope so." He heard the catch in the caller's voice. "It's Kelly Morgan and I've run into a small problem."

If she was at Lew Sterrett, he'd venture not so small.

"They think I've been drinking."

Think? Everyone in the place had been drinking. The parents of the bride hadn't pinched pennies. Not with the historic art-deco location, the food, or the free-flowing booze.

"I refused the field sobriety test."

Which meant the officer involved brought her into the station for blood tests. She didn't sound drunk to him, but he had no idea how long she'd been held in jail before getting her phone call.

"I need DJ to come here and explain that I'm not," a heavy sigh sounded through the phone, "... a drunk. They can," she sucked in a deep breath and he swore he could almost hear her swallowing. "...they can let me go home." She blew out a ragged breath, exposing the fear under the confident bravado. "Soon, please."

"We'll be there." Disconnecting the call, he scanned the large hall, then turned to his sister. "We need to find DJ. Fast."

Hannah pointed to the stairs leading down to the semi-circle reception area by the front doors. "He's coming in now."

Not waiting for his sister, he walked as quickly as was practical without drawing attention to himself and caught up with his cousin. "We've got a situation."

DJ's brows dipped into a frown. "What's happened?"

"Kelly called you." Ian handed DJ his phone. "She's been detained. DUI."

"What?" DJ's brows shot high on his forehead.

Dale, the most recent man to leave the Dallas PD, stepped up around his friend. "Where is she?"

"Lew Sterrett."

"Let's go," DJ and Dale echoed.

Ian turned to his sister and tossed her his keys. "You take my car back to the hotel. I'll meet up with you later."

"I'll follow you." Hannah leaned across a nearby table and grabbed for her purse.

"No," Dale and DJ said in unison again, before DJ continued, "Not a good idea. We'll handle it, and better not tell anyone what's going on. No sense in worrying them until we find out more."

Ian could see the argument forming in his sister's head, but with a slow nod, she agreed.

The jail was a short jaunt from the reception hall at the fairgrounds and Ian and the others were rushing through the doors in no time.

The officer at the front desk lifted his gaze as the three men pushed their way into the building. The second his gaze settled on Dale, his shoulders relaxed and a hint of something akin to friendship lit his eyes. "What brings you in at this hour?"

"Here about a friend."

The officer's head took in the men at either side of Dale, both with their badges now clipped to their belts. Focusing on DJ, the older man frowned and narrowed his gaze. "Farraday?"

DJ nodded but the smile was forced. He wasn't in a mood for small talk and Ian understood why.

This time the officer's stiff stance didn't ease as he turned to Ian's familiar Texas Ranger badge. "Who do we have in custody that warrants two former Dallas PD and a Ranger gracing us with a visit at one o'clock in the morning?"

"Kelly Morgan," DJ answered, his stance much more casual and friendly compared to the man behind the desk.

"Morgan," the officer muttered, tapping at a keyboard. "The DUI?" His expression shifted from territorial arrogance to total bewilderment.

"She's a friend," Dale repeated with a casual shrug. "Who's the arresting?"

"Cavanaugh."

From the quick bob of Dale's head that matched DJ's, Ian figured that was buddy speak for *We can work with this*.

"Can we see her?" DJ asked.

The officer's scanned each of the men then, looking at Dale, shrugged. "You know the routine."

This time Dale's grin was more like that of a man among friends. "Thanks, Jack."

From the front of the building to the lock up where Kelly and a few other misguided souls and at least a couple of working girls were kept waiting was a short walk. Even if he hadn't seen Kelly a brief while ago at the reception, she would have been easy to spot. If she pressed herself any closer to the back wall, she'd become one with it. The elation in her eyes at first sight of DJ made Ian wish someone had stopped her from driving home alone.

"You made it," she said on approach to the cold metal bars. "Can I get out of here now?" This time her faltering voice failed to hide the fear.

DJ shoved a thumb over his shoulder at Ian. "It pays to have friends in high places."

Relieved and grateful eyes turned to Ian. "If that means yes, I owe you my first born child. When I have one."

At least she still had a sense of humor. "That one won't be necessary." Especially since her freedom came at a price. For at least the next twenty-four hours, one Kelly Morgan was in his custody.

CHAPTER TWO

"This really is not necessary." Kelly couldn't be more mortified if she'd been caught running naked down Main Street in broad daylight. Even though she had indeed been completely sober, just the idea of having been taken to jail for driving under the influence, never mind being temporarily accommodated behind bars with several less than stellar members of Dallas society, made her feel like she'd totally and possibly permanently blemished the family name.

Ian Farraday hit the blinker and glanced in his side mirror. "I gave my word. It's no big deal."

If it had been no big deal, he would have allowed her to drive herself back to Tuckers Bluff. Last night, when Dale, DJ, and Ian had dropped her at the hotel, for a few short moments she thought he might actually camp out on the floor at the foot of the bed in the room she shared with his sister Hannah. He hadn't said much in objection to leaving her under her own recognizance for the night, but she could see the reservation in his eyes as clearly as she could see the Texas Ranger badge shining on his belt. When he knocked on her door bright and early this morning, letting his sister drive his precious car back home and insisting on driving Kelly's car, she knew beyond the shadow of any doubt that to him, having been released in his custody was indeed a very big deal.

Ian kept his eyes on the road. "By tomorrow morning all of this unfortunate misunderstanding will have been legally wiped away and no longer an issue."

"But until then…"

Glancing away from the road, and with that familiar Farraday twinkle in his eye, Ian flashed a smile at her. "Think of me as the big brother watching out for your virtue on prom night."

Though she'd always thought it would have been nice to have a brother, *that* was definitely not the reason why. Barely out of Dallas County limits, the ringing of her cell phone brought the conversation to an abrupt end. Rummaging through her purse, Kelly pulled out her phone and cringed. Her mother. She so did not want to explain what had happened to her last night. On the other hand, if she didn't answer her mom would simply keep calling. She sucked in a deep breath. Only DJ, Dale, Ian and Hannah knew anything about her unfortunate stint at Lew Sterret, and all four had sworn an oath of secrecy.

Kelly didn't doubt that she could trust her friends, not that she knew Dale or Ian that well, but she did know Dale adored Hannah and would do anything for her, and Ian after all was a Farraday. A Farraday's word was as solid as a bar of gold in Fort Knox. But none of that meant that her mother couldn't somehow have found out about her daughter's late-night predicament. "Morning, Mom." That sounded normal. In no way did her voice reflect the panicked woman who had spent hours in jail fretting over the possibility of some movie-like clerical error keeping her behind bars for the rest of her life. Just to make sure, she glanced at Ian.

For only the second time since they'd left the hotel, Ian turned his attention in her direction at the exact moment she looked up to him for reassurance. She seriously doubted he had any idea why she was staring at him, nor did she have any idea why he was nodding at her, but something deep in her gut believed he could read her mind and was telling her to carry on that she sounded fine.

"We're all dying to hear the whole story."

Kelly's heart sank to her stomach. The woman knew.

"How did it go?" her mom asked with a hint of enthusiasm.

"Go?"

"The wedding. Remember? The reason you drove all the way to Dallas. Was it everything y'all expected it to be?"

"And even more." Kelly held in a huge sigh of relief. But brother was last night way more than anyone had expected. "The bride looked beautiful and Finn looked prouder than a peacock.

They'll probably live to be a hundred and die holding hands."

"That's a terrible thing to say." Her mother's voice dropped a few octaves, much the way it would when Kelly had been a little girl and was being reprimanded.

"Mom, we all have to die sometime. I think passing on at the age of one hundred holding hands with the love of your life is a pretty nice way to go." Heaven knew her father's last couple of years in the semi-paralytic state after a stroke had been hard on everyone.

"Well," her mother sighed, "I suppose you have a point."

Without another word necessary, Kelly knew exactly where her mother's mind had gone to. "What have they done now?"

"Who said anyone did anything?" her mom responded a little too innocently.

Holding her breath, she waited for the other shoe to fall.

"It's just a small fire, dear."

"Fire?"

The single shaky word had Ian looking in her direction again. Her grip on the phone tightened.

"Just a little itty-bitty teeny one in the bathroom."

"The bathroom?" Kelly blinked, turning slightly away to swipe at an escaped tear.

"It was raining yesterday," her mom continued.

"The barbecue," she muttered, sucking in a long breath and blinking back any more tears. "I swear to God, you can't leave those two alone anywhere."

"Well your grandpa just wanted to show me how safe it was to start a charcoal fire in the bathroom sink. To be honest, I figured out what caused the problem at the Shady Rest."

"What's there to figure out?" Her breath caught for a fraction of a moment. "The problem was they were cooking in the bathroom."

"You know, I think the barbecue in the bathroom would have worked out just fine if they hadn't opened up the pipe under the sink to let more air in. It seems that's why the flames shot up, reaching the roof and setting the sheet rock on fire. At least this time that's when I had to get the fire extinguisher to put it out."

This time. Kelly's forehead fell into the palm of her hand. "Mom, don't tell me you stood there watching?"

Total silence was as good an admission of guilt as pleading the fifth.

"Aw, Mother."

"It's all right, dear. Frank from the café came over late last night and cut out the scorched spots and replaced the sheet rock. Later today he'll be back to texture and paint. By the time you come home you'll never know what happened."

The only way she would not know what happened was if her mother hadn't told her. Which almost made her wonder what other shenanigans her grandfather and his brother might have gotten into when she wasn't looking. Of course, she didn't dare ask. Maybe another day, but not today. She wasn't up to it. At this point she was starting to wonder about her mother's stability. It was one thing to have her grandfather, well into his eighties, a little on the daffy side. But having her mom still only in her fifties as a partner in crime terrified her. If her mom started down the slippery slope to crazy-old-coot this young, Kelly might not survive to her own crazy-old-coot stage. "Anything else, Mom?"

"No, dear, I just want to hear about the wedding."

Kelly ran her fingertips against her temple. Especially now, she wasn't up to reliving last night just yet. Not even the fun wedding part. "I'll tell you all about it over supper when I get home. Okay?"

"I suppose so. At least I know it went off without a hitch."

Without a hitch. Yeah, the wedding had. Her—not so much.

● ● ● ●

Ian wasn't sure which set his heart racing faster, the sudden pallor that washed over Kelly when she saw the name on her cell phone, or the look on her face as she uttered the word *fire*.

He didn't really know a whole lot about grown up Kelly. His brother Jamison—named after the Irish whiskey, even if his mother denied the connection because of the different spelling—was the same age as his cousin Adam. Sandwiched between them in pecking order, Ian played alongside Connor and DJ. All of them were several years older than his cousin Grace, his baby sister Hannah, and their friends Becky and Kelly. Even though he remembered seeing the girls cavorting around the ranch in the summers when the Austin Farradays would visit the Tuckers Bluff Farradays, he really didn't know this adult version of Kelly well at all. As a matter of fact, he'd probably seen her more this past year at Adam's clinic or in passing last night at the wedding than he'd seen her in the last ten or so years put together.

Truth be told, it was only the fact that she and his sister and cousin were still close friends that had him whole heartedly believing last night's arrest had to be a mistake. After some back room negotiation between his cousin, Dale, and the arresting officer, Ian as the higher statewide authority had given his word to the officer that he would make sure Kelly returned home without getting into anymore trouble or behind the wheel of the car. Dale was going to see to it that by Monday morning there would be no record of the detainment. Even though technically Kelly's release to Ian's custody had been more of a gentleman's agreement than an official action, right now he still felt very responsible for whatever happened to her, including a distressing phone call from her mother.

With more force than he would've expected from somebody as tired as Kelly seemed, she tossed her phone into her purse on the floor.

"Trouble on the home front?"

"I suppose you could say that." She unbuckled her seatbelt and shifted onto her hip to face him. "I'm living in an insane asylum."

Ignoring the blinking light on the dashboard and the urge to tell her to buckle up, Ian recognized she needed to talk and that they had several hours for him to listen. "It can't be all that bad."

"Oh really?" She twisted and yanked the seatbelt forward snapping the buckle in, continuing to stare in his direction. "My father, the sanest man I ever knew, after having been miserable with the restrictions from his stroke, died two years ago."

"I'm sorry for your loss." Those words always seemed too little too late every time he had to use them. Now was no different.

"Thank you. Then just over a year ago we found out my mom's dad had been having trouble with the senior facility he and his brother lived in. Apparently the home frowns upon old men climbing into the hot tub stark naked."

Biting back a chuckle, Ian supposed the two old men hadn't been the only ones in the hot tub. He hoped he still had it in him when he was old enough to be a grandfather.

"And the place has a perfectly good kitchen. It's why my mom and dad chose that facility for Pops and Uncle Ralph. Pops couldn't cook when he was young, there was no way anyone was trusting him with an open fire after Grams died. Shady Rest serves wonderful meals on demand in a lovely downstairs restaurant. They'll bring them to your room if a resident prefers. But no. Pops and Uncle Ralph decided they wanted grilled cheese."

"Something tells me that may not have gone well?"

Like she'd done on the phone with her mother, Kelly pinched the bridge of her nose and sucked in a deep breath. "Because small cooking appliances are not allowed in the apartments, Pops decided to follow that rule and ignore the no cooking rule. He used the iron."

If his memory served him correctly, Ian remembered more than one person in college making grilled cheese sandwiches in a pinch with an iron.

"Yeah, I know what you're thinking." Kelly sighed. "Except they put the bread between two paper towels and then set the iron on top of the paper towel and decided to go take a shower and get dressed. If it weren't for the smoke alarms they could've burned the whole place down."

The way he saw it, the old guys were adventurous *and* lucky.

"The last straw came not long after they'd sworn off meat and became vegetarians. Unhappy with barbecued brisket on the menu, they decided to grill zucchini."

Without another word Ian already had a good idea what was coming next.

"Pops is rather resourceful. Which is why he used the bathroom sink, a bag of charcoal, and a little lighter fluid. The real trouble, however, came when he removed the pipe for venting—"

"And the whole thing blew up in flames."

Kelly nodded. "That was the last straw for Shady Rest. Pops and Uncle Ralph have been living with us ever since. Most days I think corralling a litter of kittens is easier."

"So if I heard correctly, they re-created the final incident for your mother."

"Yep." She twisted around in place, leaning her head back. "The thing is, the last few months they've been behaving themselves and haven't gotten into any trouble. Playing cards with some of the other old guys in town. Talking about taking up golf again. Uncle Ralph has even gone out on a couple of dates, and then this."

The bone-weary look on her face wasn't something that a person developed from one or two events. She was tired and upset and he didn't know what to say. They'd had some challenges with his grandfather George. Most of his grandfather's life, he would take a bottle of Jameson out of the liquor cabinet in the evenings and visit different friends. It was what made him loved by so many. Unfortunately in his later years he still did that, sometimes at two or three or four in the morning. It was never easy watching the people you love grow old and confused to the point of becoming a danger to themselves. He remembered the pained feeling of loss when his grandfather had to be moved to a memory care facility for his own good. All Ian could think to do was pull her into a bear hug, much like he might a little girl who had skinned her knee, and pretend everything was going to stop hurting. Except she wasn't a little girl. Her grandfather wasn't a skinned knee. And he had no business holding her in his arms for any reason.

CHAPTER THREE

"Time for a pit stop." Riding in a caravan of cars from Dallas to Tuckers Bluff, Ian followed the car in front of them into the gas station.

Kelly glanced at the clock on the dashboard. For the last few hours she and Ian had exchanged stories of crazy grandfathers and other mishaps. More than once he'd had her laughing so hard she almost peed her pants. She truly hoped that one day she could look back at her own grandfather's antics and laugh it off, but right now she was frustrated and a little scared. Not just for what trouble her grandfather and his brother might get into, but fearful she and her mother might by sheer heredity be doomed to follow in those exasperating footsteps.

The line of cars led by Adam and Brooks with their wives, followed by the rest of the clan with her and Ian at the rear, turned one by one into the station. Kelly fished her credit card out of her wallet and hurried out of her seat to feed the pump.

Ian already had the nozzle unhooked and the gas cap uncovered. "You go on inside with the others. I'll fill her up."

"That's okay, I can do it."

"I know you can. So can I." The man flashed a full wattage Farraday smile.

What was that old expression, the acorn didn't fall far from the tree? Was there not a single man in the Farraday clan who had not inherited that ice melting smile? Through the years having been treated more like another kid sister than a friend, she'd grown pretty much immune to the inherent Farraday charms. After all, Grace's brothers felt like her own. Not so with Ian. For the first time, she truly understood the impact of the Farraday charm that all the women in town referred to. "Thank you. I thought I'd get a diet cola. Would you like something from the store?"

"No thanks. I'll be coming inside myself in a minute."

Kelly nodded, and before she did something stupid like drool or trip over her own feet, she spun around and hurried inside after her friends. The line to the bathroom was already backing up so she opted for something to nibble on first.

Standing next to Becky in the snack aisle, Hannah looked up. "What is it about long-distance driving that turns us into human garbage disposals? Everything looks delicious."

Becky chuckled. "That's because everything *is* delicious."

"And you can afford to eat every morsel." Kelly had always envied Becky's thin build. Having developed curves early on, Kelly knew the boys wanted her mostly for one thing. She'd learned how to handle that and her figure. Always managing to remain on the curvy side of the line separating full figured from overweight, or at least until recently, she thought she had.

"Unfortunately," Becky said, "no matter what I eat, I'll never have your curves. But fortunately for me, my husband likes me just the way I am." This time, like every other time her friend mentioned DJ Farraday, Becky's face twisted into a sappy grin.

Another reason why Kelly envied Becky's lack of curves. At least Becky always knew if a man showed interest, it was in her personality and not her bra size.

"You look awfully serious all of a sudden." Becky frowned. "Is something wrong?"

From slightly behind Becky, wide eyed, Hannah shook her head, silently letting Kelly know that she had not shared last night's secret.

Except Kelly's suddenly sullen thoughts had nothing to do with her short stint in jail and everything to do with the last jerk she'd dated. No matter how hard she tried to erase Brett Cunningham's biting words from her memory banks, every time she stepped in front of a mirror she had to look twice, asking herself if she really looked good, or if her choice of wardrobe made her look fat. Or worse—was Brett right and she actually was fat? She really hated him for managing in only a few months to make her question everything good she believed about herself, for making her look differently at herself. *Really*.

"It's the creep, isn't it?" Becky asked

Hannah's face folded with confusion. "Creep?"

"Yeah. The last idiot she dated—and finally unloaded. Brett was an insecure moron who got his self esteem jolt by tearing others apart. And now he's got Kelly doubting what a great figure she has."

Among other things, Kelly thought to herself. At first she'd felt special being asked out by such a successful, handsome hunk. So much so that she never noticed when his sweet attentions turned to double edged put downs; not smart, not pretty, but definitely fat.

Frowning at Kelly, Hannah looked even more confused than before. "Why would you believe him?"

"Oh Lord, please tell me we're not talking about Kelly's recent ex?" Grace came walking up the aisle. "I'm still trying to think of something I can sue him for. Sadly, the court system doesn't recognize self-centered, manipulative and controlling jackass as a suitable cause for action."

"And *Time* magazine doesn't have an edition for Asshole Ex Boyfriend of the Year either," Becky chimed in.

Hannah snickered. "So I'm guessing this guy is a controlling asshole that no one likes."

"What guy?" Ian's voice carried over Kelly's shoulder.

When she turned to face him, he frowned, except unlike his sister who was clearly confused, Ian looked more annoyed. Her stomach twisted with fear of how much had he overheard. Kelly had a feeling had he really been her big brother, her ex might have gotten an old-fashioned whooping for disrespecting her. Snapping her head back around to face her friends, she didn't know quite what to say. She didn't want him to know the ugly things her ex had said. How the guy had seen her. Right now, even though Ian was just visiting Tuckers Bluff, and was only her friend because of his sibling, she really, really, really wanted him to see her for who she'd thought herself to be only one short year ago and not through the idiot other guy's eyes. "Oh, you know," she answered with more aplomb than she felt, "just men. No one in particular. I think I'm going to buy the beef jerky. No carbs."

Her friends shuffled about, grabbing things from the shelf.

"I like the honey roasted almonds." Becky took a couple of bags.

Hannah reached over Grace's arm. "Cheddar popcorn for me. Carbs be damned."

"Atta girl." Grace reached for a second bag of kettle baked potato chips. "Carbs be damned, indeed."

Marching single file to the register, Kelly and her friends left Ian standing in the aisle. Sneaking a quick peek, she noticed he stood rooted to the floor, still frowning. It took Hannah jabbing her elbow into Kelly's side for her to look forward again. And wasn't that a new twist. Whether he sported the famous and charming Farraday smile or frowned like a territorial toddler, the guy had the same impact on her—knee buckling. She looked at the beef jerky in her hands and the popcorn in his friend's hand. Who was she kidding, no carbs wasn't going to change a thing, she should have grabbed the popcorn.

• • • •

What ever was going on with Kelly, it was enough to have the hairs on the back of Ian's neck standing on edge. Maybe it had simply been too long since his last vacation, or maybe he was merely in big brother over protective mode—not that anything about Kelly reminded him of his sister—or maybe there was more going on in her life than a misdemeanor DUI and a crazy grandfather.

"Planning on spending the weekend in aisle three?" DJ smacked his cousin on the shoulder, lightly enough to be a casual gesture, hard enough to snap Ian's attention away from Kelly.

Fingering a bag of sunflower seeds, Ian shrugged. "Just

looking for something to snack on that won't slowly poison me."

DJ's gaze traveled from the front of the store where Kelly and the others stood on line at the cashier, to the bags of peanuts, popcorn, and other typical car ride junk food neatly displayed, and back to the front of the store. "You might have better luck choosing a snack if you tried looking this way." DJ dangled a finger at the food items.

Ian wasn't fooling anyone. He should know better than to try. DJ was not that much younger than him, and both being in law enforcement had only added to the already strong bond from their youth. They understood each other, even without speaking.

"Want to tell me what's really going on?" DJ asked.

Funny, that was exactly what he'd wanted to ask Kelly. Answering DJ would be much easier if Ian had a clue why his hackles were on high alert. "I'm not really sure."

DJ looked to the cashier, only Kelly was left in line. "She *is* single."

"That's not it." Ian wasn't in the market for a woman, at least not the permanent kind. Tapping the toe of his boot behind him, he did a military turn. "Would you know anything about a sour ex-boyfriend?"

"Kelly's?"

Lips pressed tightly, Ian nodded.

DJ's gaze narrowed on his longtime friend at the front of the store. "How sour?"

"I'm not sure." Having stepped into the middle of a conversation about a manipulative, controlling ex-boyfriend— never a good combination—and though his gut told him they were talking about Kelly and someone she'd dated, he couldn't be sure. Which meant, under the circumstances, not being sure, he probably shouldn't have said anything to DJ about his suspicions. Ian knew his cousin was still unhappy that recently he'd not noticed an abusive relationship under his own nose. Which is why Ian had to ask, "Heard anything about Jake and how he and his wife are doing?"

"Fine." DJ continued to watch Kelly pay for her diet cola and beef jerky. "No more signs of violence and he's recovering quickly from the surgery."

"Good to hear. Nice to know the doctors were right about Jake's prognosis." Ian chose his next words carefully. "It wasn't your fault. You know it, I know it, the whole town knows. We can't be everywhere at all times and we can't see all things."

DJ turned to face his cousin. "Which is why you look ready to pounce at the next person who so much as looks at Kelly cross-eyed."

Quickly evaluating whether to push or give in, Ian shrugged and followed his cousin's lead. "Sometimes my gut is wrong." Not very often, but he wasn't telling DJ that part.

Shaking his head, DJ tracked Kelly on her way out of the store and toward the car, then turned back to Ian. "Last fellow she dated wasn't from Tuckers Bluff. I think she drove to Butler Springs more than he drove here, so I didn't get to observe much myself, but if anyone will know anything, my wife will. I'll see what I can find out, but I hope to hell your instincts are dead wrong on this."

He wasn't the only one. But if his gut was wrong and Kelly's personal life wasn't the problem, then what was?

• • • •

Eileen leaned left then right, stretching her back. She hadn't said anything to her brother-in-law, but she was delighted when he decided to stop for gas instead of pushing the tank to its limit and driving home in a single span. These long car rides to and from Dallas had been a heck of a lot easier on her twenty years ago. "Next time I say we drive to Abilene and fly into Dallas."

"You hate puddle jumpers." Sean Farraday unscrewed the gas cap. "Besides, it's not like we go into Dallas often."

"Doesn't matter. Whenever we go back, remind me how much my back is protesting the drive." Eileen caught sight of DJ's car pulling back onto the road and pointed. "Looks like we're not that far behind the kids after all."

"Didn't think we were. They were dancing all night too. Probably had as hard a time crawling out of bed this morning as the rest of us old folks had."

"Speak for yourself." Eileen patted the back of her hair playfully. "I'm not old yet. But too bad they didn't all sleep in an hour longer. I had hoped for an earlier start to beat everybody home." Twisting left and right, and feeling that aching tug at too many muscles, she figured she was lucky she made it out of bed this morning at all.

Strolling in her direction, his gaze going right past her, her nephew Ian didn't seem to notice her until he was practically at her feet.

"If you're looking for DJ, he just pulled out." Sean lifted his chin in the direction his son's car had taken.

"Nope. I had to use the men's room and didn't want to hold up the caravan."

"Well," Eileen shrugged, "with cell phones and GPS and emergency satellite road service, the need for caravanning is pretty much obsolete any how."

Sean returned the gas nozzle to the pump and looked up at Eileen. "Want me to get you something from inside?"

"A cold drink would be nice. Mine has gone from chilled to lukewarm to not worth a damn. In the meantime, I'm going to inspect the ladies room." Even though she'd spent the better part of the last couple of days surrounded by family, she leaned up and kissed her nephew on the cheek. It was going to be nice having him around the house for couple of weeks while Finn was on his honeymoon. "Careful driving home."

Ian smothered a chuckle and Eileen was pretty sure a few years ago he would have rolled his eyes at her too. "Yes, ma'am."

It was sheer habit after twenty plus years of worrying about her boys that had Eileen turning around by the glass door to track Ian's last steps. She was pretty sure Ian had driven to the wedding on his own after visiting his folks near Austin. And even if Eileen was remembering wrong, she didn't understand why Kelly waited for him by her car.

Eileen practically walked sideways making her way to the ladies room while keeping an eye on Ian and Kelly. Now, wasn't this an unexpected turn of events? She knew for sure that Hannah had ridden to Dallas with Kelly in Kelly's car. Which left a couple of questions. Where was Hannah, and how was she getting home? And why was Ian riding home with Kelly instead of Hannah? Curiosity winning out, she inched back toward the front door, giving her a clear view of her nephew. The man's smile bloomed wide and strong.

"I thought you were going to use the ladies room?" Sean stood beside her, a couple of cold drinks in his hands. Always a sharp man, fully aware of his surroundings, her brother-in-law's gaze followed hers and landed on the same thing she had been watching. "Oh no. Don't you let that imagination of yours run wild. There's a very logical explanation for why Ian is riding back to the ranch with Kelly."

"I'm sure you're right." And he probably was, but just in case, she scanned the edges of the property for any signs of a shaggy dog and her puppies.

CHAPTER FOUR

"Turn up this road." Kelly pointed to the last street at the edge of town. Her Dad had been raised in the town limits of Tuckers Bluff and her mom had grown up on a West Texas sheep ranch. Having met in college, the compromise for where to set up the rest of their lives had been as far out of town as possible while still being close enough to a neighbor to borrow a cup of sugar. All the homes on her street had anywhere from two to five acre lots. With one of the larger lots on the block, Kelly's mom had been content to raise chickens and grow vegetables while her dad taught history and helped coach the high school football team to the state championship two out of his twenty years of teaching.

Ian turned the corner and scanned the houses to either side of him. "I don't know that I've ever been to this side of town."

Considering how small Tuckers Bluff was, Kelly would've thought anyone who had ever lived here knew every nook and cranny. Then again, Ian and his siblings time in Tuckers Bluff had usually been limited to a few weeks in the summer and spent mostly at the ranch. "I guess now you can say you've seen it all."

One side of his mouth tilting up in an amused grin, Ian shook his head. "If there's one thing I've learned on the job it's that just when I think I've seen it all and nothing can surprise me…"

"Something surprises you."

"Yeah. That about covers it."

Kelly pointed to the two-story farm style house with a wraparound porch, two car detached garage, graying paint and one shutter on the second floor hanging precariously from a single hinge. The house looked a little sad.

"Do you park in the garage?"

Kelly shook her head. For as long as she could remember the garage was dedicated to her dad's car and the riding lawnmower. Even though they long ago had to sell her father's precious El Dorado Cadillac convertible, Kelly still parked her car in the driveway in front. "Right in front will be fine."

Ian pulled into the front semi circle drive at the same time his phone pinged with a message. Coming to a complete stop, he leaned over and looked at his cell. "It's Hannah. She's just dropped Becky off and will be leaving Meg at the B&B then she'll be here to pick me up."

Shaking her head, Kelly refrained from saying what she'd said before. At the gas station the Farradays had changed things up by divvying the carloads into men and women instead of the couples that had left Dallas. At the time Kelly had thought it made the most sense for her to ride with Hannah and the girls, but Ian had insisted on driving her all the way home. She couldn't decide if it was the stubborn chivalrous streak that ran in all Faradays, the one that assured a girl out with a Farraday would be well taken care of and brought home safe and sound, or legal responsibility, or simply male stubbornness, but she tended to lean towards the chivalry option. Not that she was technically out with a Farraday, like on a date or anything, but he was certainly making sure she got home safe and sound.

"There you are." Kelly's mom came running down the front steps and wrapped her daughter in a hug. Anyone watching would have thought they hadn't seen each other for months, instead of days. Maybe this whole grandfather thing was weighing harder on Kelly's mom than the woman was letting on.

Pulling at the arm her mother had pressing against her neck, Kelly shifted her weight. "Mom, I can't breathe."

"Sorry, dear." Her mother kissed her cheek and stepped back. "And you must be a Farraday."

"Yes, ma'am. Ian."

"One of Patrick's boys?"

"No ma'am, Brian and Anne's."

"Oh, yes." Janine Morgan extended her hand to Ian. "Thanks for bringing my little girl home."

Did her mother seriously just call her a little girl? Kelly came within inches of rolling her eyes, blowing out a sigh, stomping her feet, and telling her mother she wasn't a little girl. She hadn't been little for a long time. But of course all of that would only have proved her mother's point of view. Instead Kelly bit her tongue, smiled, and hoped Hannah would pull up before her grandfather or uncle made an appearance, adding to the family performance.

Chickens suddenly cackled loudly, her dog began barking along with a few other canines in the distance, and Kelly turned her gaze down the road, praying for Hannah to appear.

"Dag nab it, Ralph." Her grandfather Herbert's voice carried from the backyard. "I said hold it."

Through the open backyard gate, squawking with wings flapping, in a rushing wave, at least twenty chickens came scrambling toward them, her grandfather and uncle running behind.

"Oh Dad." Her mom put her fisted hands on her hips. "You tried to fix the chicken coop, didn't you? And for land sake stop chasing them."

The way Ian's eyes opened wide at the site of chickens scrambling left, right, and in every direction, he probably thought her entire family was stark raving mad.

Her mother untied her apron, and draping it like a bullfighter's cape, began redirecting some of the hens toward the back of the house. "Well, don't just stand there," she said to Kelly, but Ian was the one to spring into action. Unbuttoning his shirt, he shrugged out of it and using it the same way her mom did the apron, waved a handful of chickens toward the rear of the house.

If Kelly thought she'd been mortified last night or this morning, neither was anything compared to this afternoon's main event.

"Dad," her mother yelled, "stop chasing the chickens."

"I got one." Her uncle Ralph held a squirming chicken up for everyone to see.

Her mother turned to Kelly and handed her the apron. "You keep trying to herd the birds in the right direction. I'll man the back gate and then we can figure out what the boys did to the chicken coop."

All Kelly could do was nod; she didn't dare look up at Ian. She didn't want to know what was running through his mind. The man had to be thinking they were all completely nuts.

• • • •

Chickens. He was supposed to be helping move chickens. Not ogling Kelly's hips. Distracted with business last night, he hadn't really paid attention to what Kelly wore or how it may or may not have shown off her shape. Today, in casual sweatpants and a loose fitting T-shirt, her figure was well hidden. But with Kelly leaning forward, waving at the squawking hens, the outline of her shape was impossible to hide. A narrowing waist curved out to well-rounded hips. No matter how many times he dragged his attention back to the business at hand of moving chickens, whenever she got in his line of sight, he'd noticed something else about her. The rosy blush rising up her neck to her cheeks, the pearl-like complexion of her skin, how she nibbled on her lower lip every time a chicken ran off in the wrong direction, and heaven help him, the way her chest rose every time she blew out a frustrated breath.

"Oh my." Hannah came up the walkway giggling. "I always thought it would've been fun if Mom and Dad had raised chickens."

"You might want to reconsider that." Kelly circled around after two hens that had broken through their efforts to redirect them.

"Oh, let me try." Hannah rushed up to the two wayward chickens. Frightened by her approach both hens flapped their wings, leapt, squawked, and tore off toward the backyard.

Kelly straightened, and for the first time since the chicken scenario had begun, let out a deep laugh. "Well, that worked. They may not lay eggs for a week, but at least we got them in the backyard."

"Hey," Hannah waved her hands palm up and grinned, "what are friends for?"

By the time they finally corralled the last of the hens into the backyard, Ian was ready for a second shower of the day, and thanks to Kelly, most likely a cold one.

He secured the latch on the gate and spun about to see Kelly and her mother across the yard, shaking their heads, Mrs. Morgan waving a hammer at the two old men standing to either side of them and the gaping hole in the large wired fence area that surrounded what he assumed was the chicken coop.

"I know you were trying to help." Kelly shifted her gaze from one side of the fencing to the other then back to her grandfather.

Even not knowing the man, Ian could see the frustration in his face. Whether it was that of an aging gentleman dealing with the reality of being unable to do that which he might have easily done in his younger days or something else, Ian didn't know, but the softening look in Kelly's eyes showed she recognized it too.

"Thanks, Pop. Give me a few minutes to unpack the car and say goodbye to my friends, then we can finish fixing the fencing."

"If Ralph here had his hearing aids turned on he'd have known I said hold it not pull it." Her grandfather bent over and picked up a screwdriver and long handled pliers. "You go on and take care of your business, we'll finish up here."

Kelly opened her mouth as if ready to object, and then let it snap shut before nodding. "Okay."

The deflated look in Kelly's eyes pricked at Ian. He didn't know what to do to help her situation with her family long term, but he knew enough about ranching and fixing fences to at least help out with this little mess. "Is it all right, gentleman, if I give you a hand? I could use the exercise."

The two men looked him over from top to bottom and like a set of matching bobbleheads, nodded.

"Oh you don't have to—" Kelly's mom started

"That won't be—" Kelly's words tumbled over her mother's.

Ian held up his hand, cutting them both off. "Mrs. Morgan, you probably know my mama and Aunt Eileen well enough to know that if I don't do the neighborly thing and offer a hand, even at my age, they'll both tan my hide."

Kelly's mom let out a soft chuckle. "You do have a point. I'd better go make some lemonade."

Waiting until her mother was out of earshot, Kelly turned to him. "I won't argue, because I know you're right. But I know you didn't have to do this. Thank you."

"Need another pair of hands?" Hannah asked.

If it had been a large job he would've taken his sister up on her offer. She and Grace were as good at mending fences and ranch work as any of the Farraday men, but this was something he could've handled on his own in a short while. "I think we've got it. Thank you."

Reluctantly Kelly turned and slowly walked away with her friend. Ian looked to the two older men doing more harm than good and decided this job would take much less time if he didn't have help. No wonder Kelly was at her wits end with her aging relatives. Something told him corralling frantic chickens had been easier than keeping these men in line would be. He didn't want to even consider all the trouble these old coots, as Kelly called them, would get themselves into.

CHAPTER FIVE

"Take a look at this over here."

Ian glanced up at Connor Farraday standing several yards away from where the men had stopped for lunch. Uncle Sean had been the first up on his feet and moving with Ian only a few steps behind.

Frowning down at the recently replaced fence post, Connor shook his head. "Doesn't make any sense."

The repaired fence section looked sloppy and incomplete.

"This won't hold a newborn pup." Sean Farraday pulled his gloves from his pocket and slid them on to examine the workmanship more closely. "Unless you or your brother drank your lunch the day this was done, or Sam has been holding out an addiction to Mogen David, this wasn't done by any of us."

Connor shook his head. "That's pretty much what I thought."

Shifting around his cousin and uncle for a closer look, Ian had a good idea what had caught their attention. Usually fence line was tight and strong. This particular section was not only looser than the others, but where the ends should be tightly twisted, they appeared as though intended to be undone again soon.

His first day replacing his cousin Finn, and already Ian was faced with the secondary reason for vacationing on his uncle's ranch. Now Connor and his uncle stared at Ian for answers. He didn't need to say anything. Neither Connor nor Uncle Sean were stupid, they both already knew exactly what he was thinking. No one in the Farraday family or the Farraday Ranch had done this. Whoever had tampered with the fence line could only have one reason; they planned to return for more cattle. "Looks like somebody was dumb enough to think if they don't outright cut the fence lines, maybe local ranchers would stop noticing their missing calves."

"That's something like what I was thinking." Sean Farraday shook his head.

"This wasn't the pasture where the calf went missing is it?"

His uncle shook his head.

"Which means," Ian voiced his less pleasant thought. "It also could likely mean they're planning on coming back."

"We're going to have to have somebody keep an eye on this." His uncle waved at the rickety fence section.

Maybe. Maybe not. Ian needed to have a chat with some of the other ranchers in the area who had lost some calves. None of this was adding up. At least not to a cattle rustling ring like anything he'd ever seen before. A small part of him wished this were a real Texas Ranger assignment and his partner were here on the job with him. If nothing else, at least to bounce ideas off each other.

Sean Farraday slapped his gloves against his thigh and tucked them in his back pocket. "We've got more work to do today, gentleman."

His uncle was right. They had a big ranch to run. And now he had a new problem to solve.

● ● ● ●

Some days were easier than others. By all rights, today should've been a fantastic day. The weather was beautiful, the sun shining bright. The clinic schedule was light. Intentionally they'd booked only a few appointments after Finn's wedding, and much to Kelly's surprise there had been no emergencies. It wasn't often the entire team got to lunch at the café. Normally Kelly loved not having to shovel down a sandwich between patients or updating files. So why was she nervous as a cat in a room full of rockers following Becky and Adam across the street?

Holding the door for Becky, then Kelly, Adam frowned down at her. "You okay?"

"Me?" Kelly glanced upward at the six plus foot of Farraday brother and plastered on her best effort at an all-is-right-with-the-world smile. "Never been better."

Adam nodded, but his frown remained in place. Her boss wasn't completely convinced, and she had to give him points for caring. Of course, if he didn't care she wouldn't have a job. When her dad had suffered his stroke years ago and she'd had to come running home from college to help her mother, Adam had created the receptionist position for her and it had been hers to lose ever since. Of course, the business was much larger now. The town had grown and they were always busy. Still, she owed a great deal to Adam Farraday's generosity. The fact that he still worried about her warmed her heart.

Now if she could just get rid of the nerves that had been taunting her all day, waiting for news from Dallas, all really would be right with the world.

"Isn't this a nice surprise," Abbie called from the other side of the front counter. "Pick any spot that strikes your fancy and I'll be right with you."

The three of them settled into the booth at the end that allowed Adam a clear view of the front of the clinic. The man rarely unplugged from his job. If anyone pulled up with an emergency, he'd be out of the booth and halfway out the door before the call even came in.

"All right." Abbie came hurrying up with a pitcher of water and poured everybody a glass. "Because I know the most important thing is the pies, Frank made rhubarb and apple crumb. Special of the day is beef stew."

Becky reached for her water. "Did he make soup today?"

"Is the Pope Catholic?" Abbie chuckled shaking her head. "Broccoli and cheese."

"Good." Becky rubbed her palms together. "I love Frank's broccoli and cheese soup."

Abbie leaned forward, turned left then right, and whispered softly, "The secret is the cheese. He uses smoked Gouda."

"Whatever it is, it's the best. I'll have a bowl please." Becky sat back, a satisfied grin on her face.

"No stew?"

Becky shook her head. "Soup and apple pie, that's all a girl needs to be happy."

With her stomach in knots waiting to hear from Ian and DJ and Dale and anyone else who could tell her late night post wedding ordeal was over and done with, Kelly didn't have an appetite. "I'm not that hungry today. I think I'll follow Becky's lead and have a nice bowl of Frank's soup."

The way Abbie, Adam, and Becky remained staring at Kelly waiting for the rest of her order only reinforced what Brett had told her. She wouldn't be so curvy if she didn't eat so much. Then again, Brett was a jerk. She knew that, but might have to remind herself a few more times. She couldn't let herself buy into his malarkey. She'd come so close to believing him, so close to doubting everything about herself. She was not going to let him win.

Adam was the first to blink. His brows buckled momentarily, and Kelly knew he was debating if something was wrong again. Instead he looked to Abbie. "Since I'm not a girl, I'll have the soup and the stew *and* the pie."

"There you go." Abbie smiled. "I need more big eaters like you."

"I'm guessing that means my brothers haven't been by yet today?" Adam teased.

"Nope." Abbie turned her wrist to look at her watch. "But my guess is the word has already reached DJ that his wife is lunching here. My money is on he'll be here before I have time to serve up the soup."

No one needed to say a word in agreement. Becky grinned proudly, Adam nodded, and before Kelly could form a thought, the bell over the door sounded and DJ came through, quickly scanning the cafe. His smile broadened when his gaze landed on his wife as though he hadn't seen her in days rather than merely a few hours.

Kelly understood all the Farradays were still in the honeymoon stage of marriage, but something told her no matter how many years passed, all of her friends would still have that same sappy puppy-love look in their eyes.

Scooting into the booth beside his brother, DJ tore his gaze away from his wife, glanced in Kelly's direction and shook his head. Whether that meant bad news or no news, she wasn't sure. What she did know was that DJ had not said anything to his brother or his wife about coming to her rescue the other night or he would have outright updated her on the situation.

Juggling a large tray, Abbie appeared, and having anticipated DJ's order, unloaded four bowls of soup. "Special's beef stew," she told the police chief.

DJ grabbed onto a spoon and dipping it into the thick broth, nodded at his friend. "That'll just hit the spot. Thank you."

"Is it me," Adam squinted at his brother, "or do you look a bit frazzled?"

Swallowing the soup, DJ set his spoon down and looked to Adam. "There is a rumor in town that a local referendum is about to be presented to make Tuckers Bluff wet."

Spoons and forks clanked against dishes.

Adam's eyes rounded. "You're kidding? Booze in Tuckers Bluff?"

"I don't know. So far it's just a rumor. At least I thought so. But Mabel Berkner has spent the last forty-five minutes in front of my desk pummeling me with a barrage of reasons I'm incompetent and ungodly for allowing liquor in Tuckers Bluff."

Rolling his eyes, Adam shook his head. "That would do it."

"Do you think Mabel knows something we don't?" Kelly asked.

"If she does, she knows more than me, the mayor, *and* the City Council."

"But you're going to look into it, aren't you?" Adam picked up his spoon.

DJ nodded. "As much as Mabel and her garden club cohorts

have driven me and my predecessor insane with their nitpicking over historical preservation and acceptable paint colors, Founding Fathers memorials, and whether or not Father Tim's Wednesday night bingo is undermining the morality of the town, usually when she gets on the bandwagon she has at least some hold on reality."

"I can't imagine someone wanting to open a liquor store on Main Street." Adam stirred his soup.

Becky chuckled. "Maybe the sisters want to sell brandy for tea time."

"They probably already have a bottle stashed under the cash register." Kelly slapped her hands over her mouth and looked over to where Abbie stood behind the counter. More than once she'd known Abbie to pour a little extra something into someone's coffee if nerves needed calming. Kelly didn't want to get anyone into any trouble, even though she was pretty sure DJ knew more about it than she did.

"Either way," Adam looked at his brother, "the town has to vote on it, don't they?"

"Yes," DJ nodded. "There are at least fifteen variations of selling alcohol in the state of Texas. Listening to Mabel you'd think fifteen different establishments were going to open up with every degree of variation from hard alcohol liquor sales, to brothels serving mixed drinks, to grocery stores selling light beer."

Adam's brows inched high on his forehead. "I'm guessing the brothel was Mabel's own interpretation of the current Texas alcohol regulations."

Rolling his eyes, DJ blew out a sigh. "After forty-five minutes with Mabel, I wouldn't mind a drink no matter where it's served."

Becky crossed her arms. "Excuse me?"

Covering her mouth with her hand, Kelly hid her smile.

Adam, on the other hand, made no effort to control his guffaw. "Oh, you walked into that one, little brother."

"It's Mabel. The woman can drive any sane man crazy."

Arms laden with dinner dishes, Abbie appeared at the table. "I may regret asking, but what has that woman done now?"

"Other than test my patience? Nothing really. But if she's right and there's a referendum to allow alcohol sales in Tuckers Bluff, all hell is about to break loose."

CHAPTER SIX

Skipping out on dinner his second night at his uncle's ranch wasn't Ian's preference. In the Farraday family, mealtime was sacred. If there was something more than sacred, family dinners were it. But with only a couple weeks of vacation time, he needed to get into town to ferret out some more information on the ranches with missing calves and he didn't want to skip working the ranch tomorrow to do it.

He'd barely turned down the main road when he spotted a well-rounded derriere protruding from under the hood of a familiar parked car in front of Adam's clinic. The lights inside the clinic were out and he suspected Adam had no idea his receptionist was stranded.

Pulling into the lot by the café, he parked and trotted to the car. "Need a hand?"

"Wha…ouch."

The smack from her head striking metal made him cringe. "Sorry. Didn't mean to startle you."

Rubbing the back of her head with one hand, she looked up, squinting. "Serves me right for ignoring the idiot lights."

"Which light?"

"All of them." The surprise on his face must have shown because she immediately explained. "I was almost at the clinic this morning when the dashboard lit up. I thought it could wait until after work and a short drive to Ned's, but the dumb thing won't start."

"I see. May I?"

Wiping her hands, she stepped aside. "All yours."

It only took a few minutes to recognize the most likely problem. The alternator. "Does Ned know you're coming?"

Kelly nodded. "I called him after work."

"Good. Because I think you're going to need his tow truck."

"Really?" She bit on her lower lip and glanced back under the hood. "I was hoping it was just a loose battery cable or maybe some corrosion I could fix with a can of cola."

That made him laugh. Not so much because it was a bad idea, but because so much in day to day grime could be handled by a can of cola. And people still drink the stuff. "There's also the possibility with a couple of new belts you could be on your way."

"Oh," her shoulders straightened and her expression softened, "that shouldn't cost much."

Probably not. Even if she did need the alternator as he suspected, that shouldn't be outrageous. Ned was a fair guy, but Ian could still see the worry on her face. Hadn't the kid had enough bad luck recently? "Listen, have you had dinner yet?"

Her eyes widened with surprise, but he had no idea why. Everyone had to eat, and even though he needed to meet up with his cousin over this missing calf business, it could wait until he'd grabbed a bite.

"I…" Kelly looked down at her phone. "It's Ned. He's on his way back from towing in a trailer from Ken Brady's. Will meet me in about an hour." Her gaze met his and lovely green eyes blinked. "Guess I won't be getting home in time for supper."

"Then join me at the café?"

Those pretty green eyes widened a second time.

"Just dinner," he said quickly. Meant to reassure her that he had no untoward intentions, the way the light in her eyes immediately dimmed, he wondered if maybe he'd said the wrong thing. "Please."

Her slight nod was less than reassuring that he hadn't somehow hurt her feelings. While Ian slammed the hood of the car shut, Kelly retrieved her purse from the backseat and stood smiling in front of him. "All set."

Maybe he'd been wrong in his snap assessment. Maybe he hadn't said anything wrong. Then again, with women, what did he know?

They'd progressed only a few feet when she slowed her pace. "Is there any news on my…" she glanced left then right and whispered, "arrest?"

So wrapped up in the stretch of fence they'd stumbled on today, Dale's call earlier in the afternoon had completely slipped his mind. "Yes. I'm sorry. It's been a busy day, but everything is straightened out. You don't have to reappear in court, and there won't be anything on your record."

Only a foot away from her, he could hear the deep sigh of relief. He was an idiot for not having called her right away, or at least having made sure that DJ called her. He felt two inches tall knowing that she had been worried about this all afternoon while his mind had been on missing calves.

"Thank you so much for answering DJ's phone, and everything else. I don't even want to think about what would've happened if I'd had to sleep there all night or worse spend a few days in jail. I owe you. All of you."

Reaching for the café door, Ian smiled. "That's what friends are for."

"Thank God."

"Well there." Abbie waved. "Didn't expect to see you back in town so soon. Looks like Finn was wrong, you hold up just fine after a day's work."

Ian had to laugh out loud. He didn't know what the heck his cousins thought he did all day long in his regular job, and he would be the first to admit there were some days that were easier than others, but there were other days when he worked twice as hard as any of his cousins. Ranch or no ranch.

"Just two, expecting someone else?"

"Only two," Ian answered.

Abbie scooted around the counter. "Take any spot. I'll be by in a second with some water and to take your order."

"Make mine iced tea please." Kelly smiled at the café owner. A nice smile. Bright, sincere, nice to see.

At the table the two had barely slid in place when Abbie appeared, drinks in hand. "Special tonight is pasta puttanesca."

"I don't remember Frank making that before." Kelly frowned.

Abbie waved a finger at no one in particular. "Seems while he was helping out at your house, he and your grandpa got to talking about their time in the military. Apparently both of them spent a good deal of time in Italy. Your grandpa in the Navy, and Frank in the Marines."

"Oh boy." Kelly winced. "I hope Gramps didn't offend Frank."

"Offend?" After a short time helping corral chickens, Ian couldn't imagine such a sweet old man offending anyone. Especially someone as gruff and tough as Frank.

"I think jarhead is the kindest thing I've ever heard Gramps say about a Marine. And if I'm not mistaken, Marines don't take very kindly to that word."

"Maybe not," Abbie shrugged one shoulder, "but from what I understand they got along like a house on fire. And whatever they talked about, it's had Frank whipping up old recipes left and right. I'm just glad nobody's asked me to translate puttanesca."

This time Ian bit back a smile. One of Naples many claims to fame is their *whore style pasta*, though no one can really agree how the spaghetti sauce got its name.

"Whatever it means, I'm sure it will be delicious," Kelly nodded. "I'll try it."

"Make that two," Ian added.

"Two pasta puttanescas coming right up."

Ian waited a few moments for Abbie to walk away before speaking. "How are the repairs on the house coming along?"

"Fine. He pops over for about an hour after the café closes and does a little here, a little there. Frank does construction as well as he cooks."

"I'm not surprised. Do you know what he did in the Marines?"

"No idea." Kelly flipped her hand palm up. "I actually know

very little about him. It sounds like my grandfather may know more about him now than anybody else in town. Except maybe Abbie."

"That woman would've made a great bartender. I wouldn't be surprised if she knows everyone in town's secrets."

Kelly failed to hold back a laugh. Ian thought she had a nice smile, but he liked her laugh even more. Actually, now that he took a few seconds to think about it, there was quite a bit about Kelly he liked. Too bad he wouldn't be around long enough to do anything about it.

• • • •

Kelly didn't know where to look. She was sure every time Ian smiled at her, she probably blushed like a crushing school girl. She'd spent more time with Ian Farraday in the last two days then she had her entire life. And she'd spent plenty of time as a teenager spying on all the Farraday brothers and cousins. They'd all been off limits, but she hadn't minded getting an eyeful. By the time she'd graduated high school and gone off to college, she'd developed a healthy immunity to Grace's brothers, and she'd thought the cousins too. Until now. She may feel like a little sister around Adam and his brothers, but none of the things she was feeling right now with Ian were even remotely related to a big brother.

"Speaking of which," Kelly fiddled with the straw in her glass, "if the rumors of a referendum to sell liquor are true and the town decides to pass it, Abbie could get a lot more opportunity to listen to sob stories."

Ian shook his head. "I don't see her serving more than wine or beer with dinner."

"True." Kelly shrugged. "Still, with some folks that's all it takes."

"Honestly, with all the hoops required to jump through to get a liquor license, I wouldn't be surprised if she declares the café a

Bring Your Own Bottle restaurant"

"Hey man," Ken Brady paused at their table shoving a hand in front of Ian, "I heard you'd be around for a couple of weeks. We should hit Butler Springs Friday night."

Ian glanced up. "Maybe. We'll have to see how the week goes."

"Turning into an old man already?" Ken laughed. He was closer to Finn's age than Ian's and Kelly could see by the flash in Ian's eyes that he didn't appreciate the jab at his age. "By the way, have you heard if there's any truth to the rumor about the referendum?"

Hefting one shoulder in a lazy shrug, Ian shook his head. "Nothing confirmed."

Ken lit up like a Christmas tree. "Hot damn. Dear Lord, may we please finally get a nightspot of our own so we don't have to drive all the way to the Boots and Scoots in Butler Springs."

"I don't mind." Abbie set two plates down on the table. "You want to dance closer to home, that's fine, but the last thing I need is any competition for my dinner customers."

Ken slung an arm across Abbie's shoulder. "Tell you what, if the referendum turns out to be more than a rumor, and it passes, you clear out a few tables for a little boot scooting and a beer, and I'm all yours."

Abbie rolled her eyes and slid out from Ken's resting arm. "I may have to reconsider," she teased.

The bell announcing another patron sounded as DJ and Becky walked in. It took the man only a few seconds to scan the place and zero in on his cousin.

"Looks like we're going to need a bigger table." Kelly glanced across the café. "Are you expecting someone?" she asked Ken.

"Actually, I'm here to pick up an order. Mom's not feeling well and the last thing anybody wants is my dad in the kitchen."

DJ reached the table. "Did he start another fire?"

"Oh please," Kelly sighed, "don't mention fires."

"Sorry, Kel." DJ winced.

"No more fires," Ken answered, "and we want to keep it that way."

"Might as well pull up a chair while you're waiting." DJ pointed to the table beside them, then gestured to his cousin. "Why don't you sit on the other side so I can sit with Becky?"

"Don't make the man move." Becky moved to Kelly's side of the table.

It wasn't often she saw the town police chief pucker his lower lip in a near pout. Actually, she'd never seen the town police chief do that, but danged if it wasn't what DJ's expression looked like.

"Don't get your prize buckle in a twist." Ian pushed his plate to the empty spot beside Kelly and then slid out of the booth and settled in beside her.

Yes, she'd spent several hours in a car with the man yesterday, but there had been a console between them and she'd been more concerned over possibly being hauled back to Dallas to spend more time in jail, and what her grandfather had done to the house, rather than paying that much attention to the handsome man driving her car. Having nothing catastrophic on the horizon now left her mind wide open to notice and consider the Farraday hunk beside her.

From across the counter by the kitchen, Abbie called out to Ken. "Five more minutes and you'll be ready to go."

"Thanks." Ken slid the chair from the nearby table and hanging his arms over the back, straddled the seat. "Since we've got a few minutes, did you figure anything else out about the missing calves?"

Ian put his fork down. "Y'all have had calves go missing too?"

"Yeah. First time we noticed it we thought someone had made a mistake. Then the second calf went missing so I mentioned it to DJ to see if anyone else in the county was having trouble."

DJ nodded. "And that's what had Dad and Finn double checking the pastures."

"Which is when Grace found the downed fence line and the cigarette butts. Today we found a loosely repaired fence line." Ian waved a finger at his cousin. "I was actually coming into town to talk to you about it."

DJ turned to Ken. "Have any more calves gone missing?"

"Nope." Ken shook his head. "But my place is a fraction of the size of yours. How many calves has the ranch lost?"

"So far only one, but I put some feelers out to the neighboring ranchers to check their calf count and just a little while ago I got a call from Stan Rankin—"

"He's lost calves also?" Ian asked.

"Not calves," DJ enunciated. "Calf."

Ian threw his arms out palms up bumping against Kelly. "Sorry," he said to her before looking up at his cousin. "Who steals one cow from a ranch?"

"That would be fourteen ranches and seventeen calves over the last few months that I know of and why, dear cuz," DJ leaned back and crossed his arms, "we've got you."

Kelly shifted her gaze from her friends seated across from her, to Ken another friend since childhood, to Ian sitting way too close beside her. From the sounds of it, she wasn't the only one in town up to her armpits in crazy trouble.

CHAPTER SEVEN

"That nine is a diamond not a heart." Eileen waved a finger at her friend's cards. She'd left the ranch early for the Tuesday morning meeting after fixing breakfast and sending Sean and Ian off for the day with a packed lunch. Even though she'd skipped coffee before leaving and was barely halfway through her first cup here at the café, she could still see the mismatched card from across the table.

Ruth Ann lowered her eyes to the straight flush she'd laid out in front of her. "Damn. How did I miss that?"

Peering over the rim of her playing cards, Dorothy, another longtime member of the Tuckers Bluff Ladies Afternoon Social Club, stared pointedly at Ruth Ann. "Because you refuse to wear your glasses."

Sally May shook her head. "She's right. If Ralph walks in the door, one of us will warn you to take off your glasses."

Ruth Ann squinted at her cards again.

"Oh for land's sake." Eileen tossed her cards into the pot. They'd have to play the hand again anyhow. "Ralph won't care if you wear reading glasses. This isn't 1966. No one is going to call you Four Eyes. Heck, starting with Elton John back in the 70s and up to Lady Gaga, eyewear has become a fashion statement."

"Just get yourself a nice colorful pair with a few rhinestones and you'll look great," Dorothy said a little too happily.

"I'm not so sure if the old goat would even notice if you're wearing glasses." Sally May scooped up the cards from the middle of the table.

Ruth Ann rolled her eyes. "He's not blind and he's not that old."

"Sorry." Sally May flashed a toothy grin. "So when is the

next date?"

"I don't know." Ruth Ann sighed. "I think that fire in the sink has him distracted."

If Ruth Ann didn't look so forlorn, Eileen would have teased her at least a little bit.

Dorothy cut the deck. "I'm sure once everything is back to normal, you'll hear from him again." Unbidden, Eileen's mind dragged her back over 25 years to a place and time she'd long ago buried. Grace had just begun to pull herself up, her brother-in-law Sean had discarded all the nanny applicants, and Eileen had postponed her wedding again. Glen lost his temper and slammed the phone down hard in her ear. Anne Farraday had been nearby and noticing the pain in her eyes had mumbled something very similar, *"Soon things will be back to normal and then you'll hear from him again."*

And she had. A month later he was engaged to Sally Marshall.

"Earth to Eileen." Dorothy waved her hand in front of Eileen's face.

"Sorry. What?"

Dorothy pulled her cards close to her chest and leaned forward. "I said they've been mowing the old golf course. Have you heard of any plans to reopen?"

"Why the heck would anyone want to reopen that?" Sally May paused mid-air before slipping a card into her hand.

Dorothy shrugged. "Maybe there's some new oil business coming in. Makes sense if someone's wanting a liquor license that they may be wanting it for the clubhouse, which means they'd want the golf course playable, which means there's got to be something big moving in near town."

"That's an awful lot of *which means* and *suppositions,* don't ya think?" Ruth Ann chimed in.

"Don't know." Dorothy raised her brows high on her forehead and cocked her head with a smile. "Liquor referendum. Golf course getting mowed. It has to mean something."

"Yes," Sally May looked up from her hand, "it means rumors take on a life of their own when people start speculating. I say we play cards."

Dorothy rolled her eyes, blew out a low huff, and slumped back in her seat.

The rumor debate over, Eileen tried to focus on the cards in her hand, but her mind kept wandering back to Glen and Sally Marshall.

"Eileen!" Three faces stared at her. Clearly she'd missed another question.

"What?"

"Have you heard from Finn?" Dorothy carefully enunciated as though Eileen were demented not distracted.

"Of course not. He's on his honeymoon." What grown man breaks away from alone time with a new wife to call his aunt? Had all her friends gone off the deep end?

"Like you told Ruth Ann, this isn't 1966. The kids have cell phones with free long distance, spend more time on their apps than with human to human communication, and—"

"*Honeeeymooon*," Eileen repeated with more emphasis. "I don't care if Finn could call Mars for free."

"She does have a point." Sally May raised and lowered her eyebrows suggestively before swallowing an impish grin.

"Fine." Dorothy fanned open her cards, moving them about with a tad more gusto than necessary. "Forget I said anything."

What Eileen wished she could forget was the unopened letter that had been sitting on her dresser for weeks. *Then you'll hear from him again.*

• • • •

Ranch life started dark and early. Normally Ian would have been less than thrilled to be up even before the crack of dawn, but today he appreciated the quiet time, the hard-working time, the thinking time.

After dinner last night, he and DJ went back to DJ's office and mapped out a timeline of reported lost cattle, at least as many as they knew of. The only thing they could conclude was that these were either incredibly stupid thieves who didn't stand a chance in hell of making much money, or a brilliant masterminded ring spread a lot wider than this little piece of West Texas, amassing herds of cattle virtually undetected as stolen. His bet was on the former.

This left him spending all night mulling over possible motivation for stealing cattle. And not full grown market cows, something rustlers want, but calves. The whole thing made no sense to him, to DJ, or anyone else in the family. There was a lot of ranching background bouncing ideas around and not a single person could come up with a blessed thing.

"You're thinking about the missing cattle, aren't you?" Uncle Sean asked.

"This entire situation is one big puzzle and there are several pieces that simply don't fit."

"You're not telling me anything I don't know." Sean slipped off his gloves and stuffed them in his back pocket. "We're done with this bit of fence. I'm thinking I may want to check water levels on one of the wells that has been acting up."

"Need some help?"

"Nope." Sean Farraday shook his head. "You might as well check out our pasture with the missing calf."

Ian smothered a smile. When he was a kid both his dad and his uncle seemed to have an uncanny ability to know what he and his cousins were up to. For a few years he would've believed anyone who told them the Farraday men could read minds. Even though it made no sense now, he wasn't at all surprised that his uncle knew he'd been itching to check out the spot where Grace had found the cigarette butts. Yes, the fence had long ago been repaired, but he still wanted to see for himself. And his uncle knew it. "I'll take the horse back to the barn and take the four-wheeler out to the pasture."

Uncle Sean looked off in the direction he planned to go, then back at Ian. "Maybe I should come with you."

"Nonsense. This time we don't need an extra pair of eyes."

His uncle hesitated, weighing Ian's words. "You're probably right. I'll meet you back at the ranch house before supper."

"Sounds like a plan." Ian mounted his cousin Finn's horse. The well-trained animal responded to the barest touch. He could have picked any horse to ride and they all would prove to be excellent cow horses. Though all his cousins were fantastic with ranch animals, Connor especially work wonders with any horse from any background. Even though Ian had grown up watching his cousin's special way with all animals, especially the horses, it still surprised him just how good Connor was and how much he could accomplish.

Brandy knew the way home. Ian considered riding straight over to check out the fence line but thought better of keeping the horse out any longer. He'd barely touched ground when a brief clatter caught his attention. Hesitating, he listened carefully. Nothing. He wasn't even sure which direction the noise had come from. Brandy had been cooled, brushed, and put back in her stall when Ian heard another clatter and clunk sound and this time he could tell it came from the direction of the house.

There was no doubt that his aunt was still in town with the Ladies club, Uncle Sean was out working, and Sam and Connor were in a far pasture installing some new fence line. Neither of them was expected back until much later. So who, or what, was rattling around near the house?

Not that he really expected to find trouble, but with the possibility of rustlers in the area, and knowing all too well how easily trouble had a way of finding you, he reached for a rifle and made sure it was loaded. Keeping an empty rifle at a ranch made no sense, but he'd done his job long enough to know, always check your weapon.

Taking slow careful steps in an effort to remain as quiet as possible, he followed the direction of the out of place sounds.

Nearly to the back porch he tucked himself behind an overgrown sage bush and carefully scanned the property from left to right, taking in every window and door looking for a point of entry. Not noticing anything out of place, he surveyed the situation one more time when another louder clatter drew his attention to the east side of the house.

Unable to see from where he stood, he risked stepping out into the open and taking wider steps, hurried around to the corner and pressed himself against the siding. Tossing his hat behind him, he craned around the corner for a better look. Nothing. But something had made the noises. Then he heard it again, another clank. This time an overturned trashcan banged against the cement foundation. Immediately Ian turned his attention to the windows overhead. No sign of open glass or flowing curtains.

Ian hissed out a soft sigh. With no sign of human life, he braced himself for the other option. A critter. His aunt had been grumbling about trouble with bobcats and coyotes. Though this close to the house those were rarely a problem, he'd rather shoot a burglar or a rustler than an adventurous animal scavenging for his next meal. He really didn't like having to shoot God's critters. Now the two legged animals who deserved to fry in hell for the rest of their lives, those he didn't have a problem aiming at.

Another clashing of trash bin against wall had Ian squinting at his target. Whatever was responsible couldn't be that large. He saw no sign of angry bobcat or disgruntled coyote. So what the hell was causing this ruckus? Slowly moving forward, he kept the rifle trained at the disarrayed containers. He could see now these were the ones his aunt used for storing biodegradable trash before someone hauled it off to the larger compost pile across the yard. His mom had been forced to do the same thing when keeping discarded coffee grinds and banana peels in the kitchen brought crawly things into the house that didn't belong inside.

Without a sound, the bin already laying to its side shifted slightly away from the house as Ian came within striking distance of the culprit. Prepared for a vicious or even rabid animal, silently praying for anything but a skunk, he almost doubled over laughing when a wagging tail appeared slowly backing out of the can.

Rear end shifting in time with the happy tail, a furry pup raised his head. Catching Ian's gaze, the little guy's tail moved in double-time.

The herding mix of some kind appeared well groomed and fed. Quickly, he shifted his attention to the huge dog pen where his uncle kept the cattle dogs. He wasn't aware of any new litters, but King was almost at the age to retire so it wouldn't have surprised Ian if King had recently sired pups, and for his uncle to have decided to keep the pick of the litter. Except the pen door was closed, confirming this pup had not escaped from here.

"So who do you belong to?" Ian turned his attention back to the puppy and for the first time noticed the little rascal clamped tightly to a nice chunk of chicken carcass between his teeth. "Sorry, boy. Chicken is a no no." Ian set the gun aside and squatted onto his haunches. "Come here, boy. Let me have that."

His rear end high in the air, the little guy leaned low on his front paws and bit down on the bones.

"Don't do that!" Ian shifted forward as quickly as he could without startling the dog.

Unfortunately, the pup wasn't stupid. For a second, Ian almost thought he smiled as he raised up and trotted several feet away before facing Ian again—tail in the air, paws down—and settled in to gnaw away.

Ian had learned the hard way that cooked chicken bones and dogs do not mix. He'd been about eight years old when old Buddy stole a chicken bone from his sister Hannah's plate. A stray the family had adopted years before, Buddy had been mostly well trained. Ian's dad had done a good job of it, but regardless, Buddy still had a hard time resisting food at his muzzle's height. Hannah putting the dish down on the coffee table had been too much temptation for the old dog. He managed to gnaw the chicken bone down to a mere stub by the time they'd found him. His father gave them all a strong lecture on chicken bones and dogs, but Buddy appeared to be no worse off for his thieving. They'd been lucky, or so they'd thought. The next morning his dad found the dog in the back hall. His mom and dad told the kids the old dog had died of natural causes, and there was always the possibility that having eaten the chicken bone was a mere coincidence, but Ian had overheard his parents talking. More likely, Buddy had regurgitated the stolen chicken and choked on a splintered bone.

From stray to stray, Ian was not going to let that happen again. "Come here, fella," he said softly with a smile, inching his way forward. "How about I trade you that scrawny bone for a nice thick juicy steak?"

The dog shouldn't have understood a word he said, but nonetheless, the puppy paused, perked his ears, tipped his head sideways and appeared to be contemplating the bargain.

Not one to miss an opportunity, Ian lunged forward and grabbed hold of the protruding bones, willing to risk sharp canines if it saved the dog. Almost a game of tug-of-war, Ian pulled at the bone with one hand and scratched behind the puppy's ear with the other. It took all of a few seconds for the animal to decide that belly rubs were better than chicken, and roll over onto his back.

"Now who do you belong to? And what are you doing all the way out here by yourself?" Ian rubbed at the puppy's tummy and looked around for any sign of siblings or maybe a mama dog, not that he really expected to find one. This guy didn't look or behave like a feral dog. "We're going to have to show you to Uncle Sean and see what he thinks."

The dog rolled back upright and squirming happily, stretched his neck ready to lick Ian's face. Then he backed up, nodding his head, but it was the awful gagging sound that had Ian prying the dogs mouth open and feeling around for a caught bone. "Damn it."

Tail no longer wagging, even the puppy seemed to know this wasn't right. Continuing to gurgle and struggle, the little guy looked up at Ian and he'd have sworn the pup was reproving him for not helping.

"Looks like you're going to meet my cousin Adam before his

dad."

Cautiously lifting the dog under his arm, careful not to jar him or move the bone, making things worse, he ran through the house, grabbing keys and a nearby laundry basket and towel. Within seconds he had the dog comfortably on the towel in the basket on the floor boards of the old pickup, still gagging but thank God, still breathing.

CHAPTER EIGHT

"Yes, Mrs. Peabody, I'll make sure to tell Doc Adam as soon as he's back." Kelly had been fielding or making phone calls all day. Shortly after the vet clinic had opened the doors this morning, Adam got an emergency call from one of the ranches. He and Becky had left immediately and Kelly had been on the phone rearranging appointments all day. Thankfully most of the scheduled appointments were for some routine wellness check or vaccination updates. Only Mrs. Peabody was distraught over her cat Sadie, who was off her food and definitely not pregnant since she'd been spayed after popping out the last litter. Kelly prayed that this was another situation where the pet's owner was merely being a hypochondriac and not the one time that the poor animal actually needed Adam and couldn't wait.

Not more than five minutes had passed when the hinges squeaked on the front door. From her seat behind the counter, she could hear the sound of an animal in trouble followed by deep familiar male voice. "Need to see Adam." Ian Farraday stood in front of her, his gaze anxious, holding a laundry basket with…

"How did you get Hannah's puppy?" Already on her feet and halfway around the counter at the sound of the puppy in distress, Kelly pointed to the first exam room just up the hall.

"More like how did he get me, but whoever he is, he needs help." Ian followed Kelly into the small room.

"Where did you find him?"

Ian set the pup and basket down on the examination table. "In the compost pile at the ranch."

"At the ranch? So he's been choking for an hour?" Kelly should have said at least an hour since that's how long it should take to drive into town. She wasn't an animal tech, but she'd worked at the clinic long enough to observe and learn a thing or two. She pulled out a pen light to better see down the dog's throat.

"Yeah," Ian bobbed his head, "he's getting tired too."

Careful not to worsen the puppy's condition, Kelly lifted his chin slightly and shone the light down his throat, wishing for something she could easily reach for and remove. "I don't see anything." She scratched behind the still wheezing and gurgling dog's ears and reached for the nearby phone on the wall.

"It's going to be okay, boy," Ian encouraged.

Without looking up, the puppy thwacked his tail against the tabletop once, then twice, before it stilled.

"Adam." Kelly pushed speakerphone. "Ian just came in with Dale and Hannah's puppy. He's gagging on a chicken bone, but I don't see anything in his throat even with the light."

"How's his breathing?"

"Shallow. He's struggling. He's tried coughing it out a few times."

"He was doing it constantly at first," Ian added.

"We're about fifteen minutes out. He'll need an x-ray. Do you think you can handle it, Kel?"

She nodded, her gaze focused on Ian's large hands gently scratching the puppy, keeping him calm and then realized Adam couldn't see her. "If I run into trouble I'll go out back and get Marti to help." One of the large animal techs, Marti was doing post-op duty with a couple of the patients the doc had operated on yesterday that were still in critical condition. She hoped this fellow didn't come to that.

"Atta girl. Are Dale or Hannah there?"

"No. It doesn't sound like they know he's hurt."

"All right. We'll give Hannah a quick call. Just keep him as calm and still as you can until I get there."

"That's the plan." Kelly hung up, running all the times she'd helped with x-rays through her mind and almost smiled at the soothing gentle attention Ian showed the worn out pup. "Looks like he'll give you another hour or two to stop that."

"No kidding." He flashed her a hint of the famed Farraday smile.

"If you don't mind, I'll carry the basket, you just keep scratching his ears and chin."

Ian nodded. She was a little surprised at his willingness to follow her instructions. Not that she expected him to be unreasonable, but it seemed that lately the only kind of man she ran into were the ones who balked at following any suggestion, never mind orders, given by a woman.

Everything set in the other room, keeping the dog still long enough to get a decent picture had been much easier than she'd expected. Too easy. Kelly didn't like it one bit. Rather than move him again, she opted to wait in this room for Adam. "Poor fellow." She gently rubbed his side as Ian continued to scratch by his chin. The puppy struggled to breathe but had given up on trying to cough up the bone, and staying perfectly still, whimpered softly.

"He's such a sweet pup. I hate to see him suffer." Ian alternated from scratching behind the dog's ears to under his chin and back.

Once again the front door squeaked open followed by the sound of pounding heels coming up the hall.

Adam came through the door first. "How's he doing?"

"He seems calmer," Ian said.

Immediately Adam approached the injured animal, quickly evaluating the situation. "Let's look at those x-rays."

Becky placed the x-rays on the lit panel as Adam added, "Couldn't get a hold of Hannah, but Dale is on his way."

"Here's the problem."

As many x-rays as Kelly had seen, she was still surprised she could clearly recognize the jagged outline of the small bone caught low in the puppy's throat.

"And here." Adam pointed to the additional x-ray Kelly had thought to take of the animal's abdomen. "This fragment has perforated the bowel causing internal bleeding. We'll have to prep him for surgery."

"Then he'll be okay?" Ian asked.

Adam patted his cousin on the shoulder. "I hope so."

Filling the hall, Dale's voice grew louder as he approached the x-ray room. "Got it. Okay. Love you more."

From the face splitting grin, it was obvious Hannah had been on the other end of the cell. The second his gaze fell on the lethargic puppy, the smile disappeared. Dropping his phone into his breast pocket, he crossed the small space in only two steps and joining his cousin, began gently scratching the scruff of the puppy's neck. "I don't know who this little guy is, but our pup is at the arena with Hannah."

• • • •

A stunned moment of silence passed as it registered with everybody that a new puppy had worked its way into their lives. Well, Ian's life.

"We'll have to worry about who he belongs to later." Becky nudged her way between Kelly and Ian, hovering over the puppy. "Time to get cracking."

As Adam and Becky hurried out the door to the OR, a heaviness pressed against Ian's rib cage at the thought this could be the last time he saw the puppy. In a little more than an hour somehow he had managed to grow very attached to the four-legged fur ball. Not until Kelly lightly laid her fingertips against his elbow and nudged him forward did he realize he'd stood almost paralyzed in place.

"I'd better send a message to Uncle Sean and let him know I'm going to be a little longer getting home."

"You don't have to wait here. Adam will take good care of him and see that he's comfortable. I'll put the word out to see if we can track down who that pup belongs to."

Dale followed the two out of the x-ray room. "Don't be surprised if you don't find anybody."

"What do you mean?" Ian looked over his shoulder.

Shrugging, Dale raised his eyebrows. "I'm just saying, this puppy looks enough like our dog to be a litter mate. And if that's the case, then the dog doesn't belong to anybody. Except maybe his parents. And that mystery has yet to be solved."

"Mystery?" Ian asked

Kelly stuttered to a stop. "You think he belongs to the strays?"

"I haven't a clue. I'm just guessing here." Dale shook his head. "I'm off duty in about an hour. I'll pop back and check on him. Let me know if there's any news before that."

"Will do," Kelly said.

The front door closed behind Dale and Ian turned to the woman beside him. Her gaze lingered off into space, her intense focus on some unknown point. "You're worried, aren't you?"

"Hmm?" She pivoted to face him.

"You look worried. It's that serious, isn't it?"

She blinked a couple of times, then shifted her attention down the hall to the OR and back. "Maybe not."

"But you are worried? I can see it in your eyes."

"Oh. Not really. I was just lost in thought a moment."

A small part of him was delighted that she didn't fear the worst for the puppy, but another part of him already didn't like whatever situation or circumstance had her looking so distraught. "Anything I can help with?"

Shaking her head, whether in response to him, or physically trying to rattle away unpleasant thoughts, she took a step back and forced a light chuckle. "No. I guess I was just contemplating the immortality of the crab."

The not often used expression reminded him of his Aunt Helen. It was one of those things she always said to the kids whenever they asked her what she was thinking about. It had been a horrible blow for a young boy when he finally understood that he'd never see her again. The loss had been hard enough to take, but he couldn't even begin to fathom the hurt his cousins had felt. The entire family had been incredibly fortunate that their Aunt

Eileen had stepped into her sister's shoes without skipping a beat. Which reminded him that she was across the street playing cards. "I'd better call Aunt Eileen and let her know what's going on too."

Chuckling, Kelly lifted a finger and pointed out the window. "That won't be necessary. The Tuckers Bluff emergency broadcast system has clearly been put into effect."

With the intensity of a general leading his troops into battle, Aunt Eileen led the card playing posse across the street and straight to the clinic door. He barely managed to contain his own laughter as the four women paraded into the front room.

"You should've called us." Aunt Eileen pushed onto her tippy toes and kissed Ian's cheek before turning to Kelly. "Is he still in surgery?"

Kelly nodded. "Adam and Becky just took him into the OR barely a few minutes ago."

"Is he really from the same litter as Dale and Hannah's puppy?" One of the women asked.

"We don't know," Ian answered

Becky's grandmother—Ian had forgotten her name—inched around his Aunt Eileen. "But he does belong to the town strays?"

"We don't know that either," Kelly answered a little more sternly then Ian expected.

Arms crossed, her mouth tilted up in a knowing smile, Sally May looked to his aunt. "Put me on record now ladies, my money is on that puppy being from the same litter."

Eyes slightly narrowed, Aunt Eileen looked from Kelly to Ian and then back again. He was almost willing to swear to a judge and jury that she was searching for something. Dilated pupils, loose lips, drunken imbalance, something. Either she did or didn't find what she was looking for, but either way, it must have made her happy, because a large grin spread across her face and she nodded. "I think it would be real nice if those puppies were related."

"Is the puppy gonna make it?" a tall gray-haired woman asked.

Ian was going to have to visit town more often. On the tip of his tongue, he couldn't remember the gray-haired lady's name.

Shaking her head, Kelly blew out a heavy breath. "I couldn't say."

"Well then, ladies," Aunt Eileen turned, "I'd say we have a seat and wait to see how this turns out."

Kelly looked from Ian to the older women, let out the barest of sighs—one he was pretty sure only he had noticed—and smiled. "If you'd like to return to your game, I promise to call as soon as we know anything."

The way the four women looked back and forth, shrugging, frowning, struggling with the decision, he would've thought it was a human loved one undergoing the knife and not a small animal they had never seen before.

Aunt Eileen was the first to nod at Kelly. "Makes sense, dear."

To Ian, Kelly's smile looked a little shaky, but she held it until the last of the ladies had crossed the threshold.

Every investigative instinct he had told him there was much more to the conversation that had just ensued than mere concern for a stray puppy. No matter how much he loved his aunt, or liked Kelly, or the other ladies for that matter, there was only one thing he was sure of. Whatever had just happened was none of his business.

CHAPTER NINE

T alk about dodging a bullet. Even after the newest addition to the Tuckers Bluff police force mentioned that the clinic's new patient wasn't the puppy who had adopted him and Hannah, the connection between the puppies, the stray dogs, and the town rumors hadn't fully sunk in until Aunt Eileen's comments.

The last thing Kelly needed right now was for one of the social club ladies to start talking about rumors and mysterious matchmaking dogs. Especially since it was obvious they believe the new generation of matchmakers might be cute puppies. Not that she had any objections to being matched with Ian Farraday. Not only was he easy on the eyes, the guy was really nice. Actually, for a guy he was unusually nice. Of course, he *was* a Farraday. So far all the Farradays she had ever met seemed to be a breed unto themselves. Handsome, polite, family minded, gentlemen—and brother were those hard to find nowadays—and all with just a touch of knight in shining armor.

A few nights ago Ian Farraday had certainly been her knight in shining armor. Not that her cousin DJ and his friend Dale might not have been able to do the same, but Ian's Texas Ranger badge had definitely been the dealmaker in keeping her out of jail. Even so, saving her hide and being her perfect match were two different things. Besides, even if he were her perfect match, he didn't live anywhere near Tuckers Bluff. A TV camera worthy, good-looking guy like Ian didn't fall for curvy, big boned girls like her. Especially not if half the town descended on him like an old West posse rambling on about matchmaking puppies and destiny. Farraday or not, there was one thing about men Kelly was absolutely sure of. The last thing they want to do is what somebody else insists they *had* to do.

"Are you sure something isn't wrong?" One brow cocked higher than the other, Ian studied her curiously.

"You got me." She tried smiling. "I guess I am a little worried about the puppy." And before this guy read through her lie, she turned toward the hallway and asked over her shoulder, "I think I'll get something to drink from the fridge. Would you like a glass of water or cola, maybe hot coffee or tea? I can do either but we're out of creamer."

"Water would be nice, thank you."

For just a moment she thought he was going to follow her. Now she could add paranoid to her list of recently exposed flaws. He would probably laugh off the town theories as nothing more than superstition. Being linked with her by town rumor probably wasn't even a sliver of an idea in the deepest recesses of his mind. The truth was she was having a harder time shaking off the stabbing words her ex had snapped at her than she should. Grabbing a diet cola and bottle of water from the fridge, she lifted her chin, straightened her back, and decided to put on her big girl panties and forget about town rumors and figure out what to do with this puppy if it came through—no—*when* it came through surgery.

A bottle in each hand, she took a peek through the small window on the surgery room door. Only able to see the doc still working on his patient, she turned on her heel, sucked up every ounce of good sense she possessed, and returned to the waiting room. Painted with concern, Ian almost stole her breath, every fortifying inch of it. Maybe if she didn't react so absurdly every time she looked at him, she wouldn't care so much what crazy ideas the afternoon social club might or might not spread. "Here you go."

"Thanks." Still standing, Ian offered a tired smile.

Good thing too. In the crazy mood she was in Kelly wasn't sure she could handle a full-watt Farraday smile. "I peeked into the operating room, but all I could see is that Adam is still working on him.”

Ian nodded, unscrewed the bottle cap, and took a quick chug. “I suppose it’s a good sign that he’s holding his own during surgery.”

“Yeah, that’s what I’m telling myself.” Kelly mindlessly fidgeted with the cap on her cola. “Puppies have a way of getting into all sorts of things they shouldn’t. Usually the dogs will just pass strange things. We’ve had pet owners waiting to retrieve treasured jewelry, valuable coins, or the only key to a locked door. Other times Adam has to go in and surgically remove something.”

“Like this little guy and his chicken bones.”

“Exactly like that. Only last week Adam had to go in and remove rocks from an overly inquisitive Labrador’s stomach. Now the challenge for the owners is how to keep him from digging them up and swallowing more.”

“That the Lab came through and is doing well is encouraging.” Ian’s smile held more sincerity.

Kelly nodded, but she wasn’t going to mention the Labrador had not been bleeding internally. His was more of a digestive issue, no real risk of bleeding out or a fatal bout of peritonitis from the puncture wound.

Turning slightly, Ian waved at the empty seats behind him. “We might as well sit while we wait.”

“I should try to get some work done.”

Offering a curt dip of his chin, Ian kept his gaze on her. “Of course.”

For a few silent moments they each seemed to be waiting for the other to move first. Ian took a half step backward and Kelly had to restrain herself from following him with a half step forward, but she didn’t make a move toward her desk either. All she seemed to be able to focus on was Ian standing straight and strong in front of her.

His gaze wandered from her to the door at the end of the hall. “I wonder how much longer it will be?”

Dragging her thoughts away from the Farraday cousin, Kelly

stared off in the same direction. "Not long, I hope." She knew the longer it took the more damage the splintered bones will have caused.

As he shifted his attention back in her direction, their gazes collided and held long enough for her to see her own concern reflected in his eyes. Who was she kidding? If she glued herself to the seat behind her desk, she still wouldn't be able to concentrate on anything except what was going on behind the closed doors and the man as worried about it as she was. "Maybe I'll have a seat after all."

• • • •

Fifteen or so cows of varying sizes, depending on if they came from fall or spring calving, huddled under the lone shade tree, an occasional *moo* breaking the otherwise peaceful day.

"We're going to have to do something. Can't keep hiding them here forever."

His partner in crime had a point. One he'd been gnawing on for weeks now. He'd known after helping themselves to that last calf from the Farraday spread that he needed to come up with a new plan. A more practical one that helped them reach their goal.

"If this little herd of ours keeps growing, it won't be long before someone starts asking all the wrong, or right, questions."

He hated it when people stated the obvious, or more precisely, when they stated the obvious and assumed he had no idea on his own. "Yes. I get it. And I'm going to come up with something. I just need a little more time."

"Well," the frustrated man stomped a cigarette into the ground, "better not waste much more of it."

"And you need to quit sucking on those death sticks." Time, or lack there of, was something he did not want to be reminded of. His hands, or thoughts, were already full of too many problems.

"I'll mind my business and you figure out what to do with all these cows." Having taken two steps toward the trough, his associate turned to face him. "Sooner would be better than later."

Like he didn't already know that.

• • • •

The slight brush of Kelly's arm against Ian's as she took a seat beside him caught him by surprise. Not so much the touch, but his reaction. Her warmth pierced his skin, soothing his concerns and worries like his mom's ginger honey tea soothed a cranky cold. The feeling left him startled, unsettled and smothering a contented smile. And he had no idea why. She wouldn't be the first or last woman to accidentally bump against him and yet the simple fact that he was hyper-focused on a single touch and its power to affect his mood made him nervous enough to contemplate how it would look if he moved a few chairs over while waiting. Ridiculous had been the first word to come to mind. He wasn't a hormonal teen with uncontrollable impulses, he was a fully grown, well trained law enforcement officer who could certainly sit next to an attractive woman and wait for news on the stray without doing something stupid—like run his finger along the curve of her jaw and see if another touch gave him the same jolt.

"He really seems awfully sweet for a stray," Kelly mumbled, her gaze focusing on the empty hallway.

Her voice snapped Ian out of his own thoughts. It took a few seconds to process what she'd said before he could answer. "Suppose he hasn't had time to be disappointed by the outside world and turn fearful. Besides, dogs are pack animals, stray canines adapt to people better than a feral cat might."

"True." She frowned and turned to face him. "But if he's a stray, I wonder why he looks so well fed?"

"His mama." Ian wondered why she hadn't been anywhere nearby.

Kelly hefted her shoulder in a lazy shrug. "He seems old enough to be weaned."

That was what he thought also.

"Still," Kelly hesitated, "if he doesn't belong to anybody, once he comes out of the anesthesia and is deemed strong enough to go home, he's going to need a place to go."

Again, he and Kelly's minds had gone in the same direction. At least about the puppy. The ranch might be able to use another cow dog. Not that he had any idea if the dog would be any good with cattle. Though there was a sharpness in the pup's eyes that told Ian somewhere in his background was a good smart breed. Not that it mattered, the gleam in Kelly's eyes told him that she already had a plan in mind and it had nothing to do with learning to be a cattle dog at the ranch. "You're thinking of taking him home, aren't you?"

A sweet smile bloomed on her face. "We have a house, lots of land. Of course, I'd have to talk to my mom."

"You think there's a chance she'll say no?" He had to pull his mind away from running his fingers across that sweet smile.

"Honestly, things have been so crazy since Pops has been staying with us that I haven't a clue if Mom thinks having a dog around will be a fun distraction or just one more thing to keep track of."

The door swung open to the OR and Adam strolled through sporting a telltale huge grin. "It's all good. We'll keep him overnight just to be sure. But if he stays away from chicken bones he should be fine."

Kelly flung her arms around Adam's neck and squealed, "Thank you."

"Watch it." Becky came down the hall waving a finger. "I know his wife."

Spinning about, Kelly pulled Becky into an equally enthusiastic hug. "That's okay. I'm an equal opportunity hug—"

The loud quips of a barking dog cut her words off. Closest to the window, Ian took a single step back and turned to glance in the direction of the barks.

Over his shoulder, Adam's gaze landed on the culprit and his mouth tipped upward in a knowing smile. "Well, I'll be."

A gray wolf mix sat on the curb, tail wagging. One paw held up slightly made an upward motion before setting back down on the ground and she let out another short bark. If Ian had to make odds, he'd say the animal was happy and saying thank you. "My guess is we found mama, but how the heck did she find us?"

CHAPTER TEN

*O*h *lord, now what?* Standing on the curb alongside the Farradays staring up and down the street in search of the once again missing mama dog, Kelly braced herself as her mom came marching up to the front door of the clinic. Her mother never stopped by during a work day, this couldn't be good. Forcing a pleasant smile, Kelly pushed aside visions of her grandfather starting bonfires in the living room or chasing chickens down the street. "What brings you by in the middle of the afternoon?"

Her mom lifted her arms, holding a shopping bag in each hand. "Picking up a few things for my trip."

"Trip?" Her mother never went anywhere. If she had a trip planned, Kelly would know about it. Should know about it.

"Yes, dear." Her mother turned to Adam, Becky, and Ian. "Any word from Finn and his new bride?"

"No ma'am," Adam answered, holding back a wry smile.

"Good." Her mom sprouted a broad grin. "Would have been a little worried if you had."

One corner of Adam's mouth tipped higher in a knowing smile. "Yes ma'am."

Like a matching bookend, standing across from her mother, Ian's lazy smile matched his cousin's.

"If you'll excuse me," Adam turned back towards the office, "I need to return to my patient."

"Since I'm in town," Ian took a step in retreat, "I'm going to stop in and see DJ,"

Becky's head bobbed in agreement. Taking one last glance up and down the block, she shrugged and turned toward the clinic.

"We might as well go inside too." Placing her hand on the

small of her mom's back, Kelly nudged her toward the clinic door. As soon as they crossed the threshold, she turned to face her mom. "What's all this about a trip?"

"Well." Her mom's face scrunched in thought before relaxing into a smile. "I don't know if Houston counts as a trip exactly, but Marilyn called me this morning. There was a last-minute cancellation for a class she was signed up to take in Chicago and needs to complete by the end of this month, so her company registered her to take the class in Houston instead. It's been a few years since I've seen Marilyn. She's got a free extra bed in her hotel room. How could I not take advantage of that?"

Her mother had stayed surprisingly close to her college friends through the years, especially with Marilyn, but they hadn't had any face to face time in years. "That's always a nice perk. When are you going?"

"That's just it. She's already there. I'll be flying in first thing in the morning."

"As in tomorrow morning?" A taste of panic crept up Kelly's throat at the thought of no one being around to keep an eye on her grandpa. Except her.

"That's right. Marilyn will be done with her portion mid day and because she needs to attend one Monday session, she gets two whole days in Houston paid for by the company with nothing to do."

"And you're going to take care of keeping Marilyn busy." Part of her wanted to scream *No don't leave me*, but the part of her that loved her mother very much couldn't object. "Do you have a ride to the airport?"

"Yes, your grandpa's going to take me."

Panic now had a crushing grip around Kelly's windpipe. "Gramps shouldn't be driving around town, never mind all the way to Midland airport."

"Your grandfather may be a little adventurous, a little forgetful, and maybe even a little quirky, but driving from here to Midland isn't exactly like driving from New York to LA. We'll be fine."

And it was exactly that attitude about her grandfather that gave him enough leeway to get into so much trouble. "I'm sure if I ask Adam, he'll give me the morning off to drive you in myself."

"Nonsense, Adam is a wonderful boss, but save the requests for extra time off for something you really need. We don't want to take advantage of his good nature. And besides, we'll be fine."

Kelly resisted the urge to argue. What constituted fine, like beauty, too often was in the eye of the beholder. "When will you be back?"

"I'm not sure; we're going to play it by ear. If nothing important creeps up at her office by Monday morning, we thought we'd take a few extra days and do a little sightseeing."

Heaven knew her mom deserved a few good days of fun with an old friend, but Kelly merely wished the ideas of handling her grandfather, her uncle, and possibly a new puppy weren't already so overwhelming, and her mother hadn't even left yet. Which brought her back around to the dog. "Mom?"

"Yes?"

"We got the cutest new patient today."

Her mom nodded.

"A puppy. Maybe a shepherd mix."

"We have a lot of those in these parts. Australian shepherds, German shepherds, all good cow dogs."

"Yes well, this one choked on a chicken bone."

"Oh no." Her mom lifted both hands, palms flat against her chest. "Poor little thing."

Sympathy was exactly what Kelly was going for. Combine cute, sweet, and pity, and she might just be able to take the puppy home with her. "I was just going to go check on him. Why don't you come with me?"

"Well at least he's okay," her mom muttered following behind her. "Careless people shouldn't be allowed to have dogs. Everyone knows chicken bones are bad for them."

"That's just it." Kelly pushed the OR door open and

continued back to the recovery room where Adam and Becky stood over the still sleeping pup.

"Oh, he is adorable!" Kelly's mom stretched her hand forward and scratched under the puppy's chin.

"He's a stray." Kelly smiled.

Her mom chuckled, shifting her hand to rub behind his floppy ear. "I should've seen that one coming." Looking up at her daughter, she shook her head with amusement. "When does he come home?"

Kelly threw her arms around her mom in a tight hug. "I hoped you were going to ask that."

"Could be as early as tomorrow," Adam answered.

"Oh my." Kelly's mom took a step back straightening her shoulders. "I'd better make a stop at Sisters and the feed store."

"You don't think it will be too much with Pops and Uncle Ralph?"

"Nonsense," her mom waved her off. "If anything, training a dog will give them something safe to do."

Safe? She supposed her mother was right. How much trouble could two men get into housebreaking a dog? Then again… "Don't worry about the store. What we don't have here, I'll pick up."

"You sure?" her mom asked.

Kelly nodded. "You just get ready for your trip, Mom."

"Love you, baby." Grinning from ear to ear, her mother gave her a tight squeeze, waved at Adam and Becky, and hurried out the door, a spring in her step.

"That went well." Becky gave her friend a thumbs up. "If you hadn't spoken up, I was going to talk to DJ."

Adam shook his head. "And I was going to talk to Meg."

The three of them chuckled.

Kelly rolled her eyes skyward. "Good thing we don't get a lot of strays in here."

"The place would be more like Noah's Ark," Becky agreed.

Right. Like Noah's Ark. Two by two. The little guy looked so sweet. The soft-sided cone Becky had snapped around his neck for when he woke up looked to be as big as he was. Maybe bigger. Maybe once they're all set up and the puppy is feeling better, she should look into a companion playmate for him. A good idea. One that had her wondering if there were any more pups in his litter, and had that really been mama outside the clinic? It was almost as if she'd given her stamp of approval, much the way the parents had done with Hannah and Dale, but would she be happy to know Kelly was taking this guy home to her crazy family? Or was she the crazy one even considering the mama dog was picking out parents for her pups?

• • • •

Arms laden with supplies, Ian felt a little silly showing up at the clinic again so soon, but his mind had wandered to how the puppy was doing and paid little attention to his conversation with DJ. At least picking up a few things made him feel like he was doing something. The bright smile that took over Kelly's face when her gaze fell on him made the shopping trip more than worthwhile.

"You've been busy." Kelly stood and walked around to greet Ian.

"Ran into your mom on her way into the Cut and Curl. She mentioned that you'll be taking the dog home tomorrow."

Prying a bag open with her fingertip, Kelly peeked at the contents and nodded.

"I hope you don't mind, I picked up a few things."

"Oh look at this." Kelly pulled out a huge rubber bone and laughed. "No splinters."

"That's what I was thinking. You stuff one end with something like peanut butter or cheese."

"Yeah, they're really popular with dogs that like to chew." Taking one of the bags from him and setting it down on the desk, she glanced at the large bed under his arm. "Let's take this back to where he's resting."

Ian nodded and followed her down the hall. "Adam with

him?"

"No." She pushed the swinging door open. "He was beat. Went home early. Becky too. There's a tech coming in late tonight who will keep an eye on him till morning. I'm going to stay with him till then. Becky's just upstairs if I need anything, but he's mostly going to be sleeping off the anesthesia."

Only one of the kennels along the rear wall had an occupant. From his approach into the room, Ian could see the puppy was still pretty lethargic. "Rest is good for him." Not until the lifeless tail gave a single thwack against the hard surface at the sound of his voice did Ian even realize the little guy was not sound asleep.

Even though he was a small dog, Adam had placed him in one of the larger kennels. The little fellow lay curled up on a hammock raised a few inches off the ground.

"Hey buddy," Ian cooed, stepping into the large space.

The dog pushed upward. Awkwardly lifting his head, he struggled to wiggle off the bed.

"Is he supposed to do that?" Ian asked.

Kelly squatted and dropping the new dog bed on the ground, reached over to pet and soothe the tired animal. "He needs to take it easy, but he's okay."

Head hanging over the side, the moment Ian reached forward to scratch his neck, the dog dipped his chin and licked at Ian's hand.

"Bet that's a thank you." Kelly smiled.

Settling down on the ground in a traditional lotus position, Ian stroked at the dog's side, looking carefully at the shaven belly and ugly stitches.

"Don't worry," Kelly raked her fingers along the pup's hip. "His fur will grow back and cover all the scars."

"I wish I'd gotten to him a few seconds sooner."

"At least you got to him. Had he run off with that bone into an empty pasture or field, he would eventually have died alone."

The accuracy of the prediction wasn't doing much to make Ian feel any better about not having found the puppy sooner to stop him from chomping on the bone.

"Any more sign of the mama dog outside?" Kelly asked.

Ian shook his head. He'd wondered about her too. From what Esther at the station explained, this and another dog had a reputation for appearing and disappearing at will around town. He'd heard tidbits here and there about the matchmaking dogs, but before Esther could fill in the details, DJ had called him into his office.

For a few peaceful minutes, Kelly and Ian sat side by side, each stroking a different section of the furry pup until with a wormlike shrug, the dog pushed himself forward and plopped over onto the two. The bulk of his body curled into Ian's lap, his head and front paws draped over Kelly's.

"I don't think he likes sleeping alone." Kelly rubbed her knuckle at his jawline. "I bet he sleeps with littermates. Or his parents."

"He wouldn't be the first toddler to sleep with his folks."

"No," Kelly smiled, a pretty, sweet smile. "I don't suppose he is."

"The thing that always amazes me about these animals is the unconditional love."

"I know. Doesn't matter what their masters say or do. They're always devoted." Kelly's eyes remained fixed on the dog. "Don't you wish people could be more like dogs?"

Something in her face told Ian the comment was not as off handed as it might have been coming from someone else. "I know a few who could learn a lesson or two."

"This guy trusts us to take care of him. To be kind. And I bet he'd never turn around and bite us."

"Not on purpose." Ian wished he knew Kelly better, then he could come right out and ask what was bothering her the way he would Hannah or Grace. Not that either would tell him. Most of the time he'd get some mumbo jumbo answer that he was positive had nothing to do with the truth and everything to do with why he would never fully understand women. Except right about now, watching the sadness deepen in Kelly's gaze, he really wished he knew the right thing to say. "What's really on your mind?"

CHAPTER ELEVEN

"**M**en," she muttered before the filters in her mind could stop her. The second she heard her own words her eyes almost popped out of her head and her free hand flew to her mouth in an effort to stop her from saying anything else stupid.

Based on the hint of a smile teasing at the corners of Ian's mouth, Kelly was convinced she had completely succeeded in making a total fool of herself.

Letting her hand drop, she opted to scratch the dog's ears with both hands. "I didn't mean that the way it sounded."

"What did you mean?"

Her heart racing at double time, she forced herself to lift her gaze from the dog to Ian. No hint of a smile remained. He continued to slowly run his hand along the dog's side but kept his eyes steady on her. Right now she'd pay big bucks to know what he was thinking.

Silence hung between them until it was clear Ian had no intention of saying anything else until she answered. Sucking in a long breath and then blowing it out in resignation, she shrugged. "Let's just say my last relationship didn't go so well and I'm probably better off with the dog."

"You don't really believe that, do you?"

She lifted her shoulder in a lazy shrug. "It's hard."

"Which part?"

"I've never been the skinny, pretty girl. Growing up, on the playground during school, Grace and Becky were the pretty ones, the normal ones." She glanced at Ian's direction, noticing a small frown forming between his brows, but he said nothing. "At first I remember parents, neighbors, even teachers sometimes saying I just had to grow out of my baby fat."

The frown remained on Ian's face, but this time he bobbed his chin in a curt nod.

"Then I," she swallowed searching for the right words, "blossomed. And I started getting lots of attention, but even as young as I was, I knew it was for all the wrong reasons."

This time Ian's mouth pressed into a thin line as he considered her words.

"By high school everybody had filled out more proportionately. I wasn't such a standout anymore, but I was still the only curvy girl in class." She huffed a halfhearted chuckle. "At least I wasn't told I had baby fat anymore. I'd become curvy and big boned."

"A lot of women pay big bucks for curvy."

She nodded. "True, but still, we always want what we don't have. Becky spent most of her adult life telling me she'd kill for my curves, and I'd have killed to be looked at first for anything besides my figure." Kelly wasn't going to tell him that she also would've killed to have had a good honorable man like DJ Farraday fall head over boot heels in love with her no matter what she looked like. "Anyhow, in the long run I finally realized most men are jerks." She winced. "Sorry, no offense intended."

One side of his mouth tipped up in a Farraday smile. "No offense taken."

"And I learned to recognize the nice normal ones. A few were really nice guys, and are still friends. It's just this last one. Brett. Tall, thin, strong shoulders, bright blue eyes, the kind of guy you'd see on a romance book cover. The one all the girls dream of. At first I was so flabbergasted that somebody so nice and good-looking was interested in me that I think I was a little blinded to some of his not so nice flaws."

That little frown reappeared between Ian's brows.

"Becky was the first one to notice the little digs. Then Grace. Not until Joanna asked me why I put up with the jerk did I realize he *was* a jerk."

Ian had stopped stroking the dog. She could see the tension building in his shoulders and filtering down to the stiffness in his fingers. The hand at his side curled into a loose fist and she realized what he must be thinking.

"He didn't hit me or anything like that. I wouldn't put up with anybody that stupid. It was just the subtle remarks about what I was wearing. How this skirt made my butt look big. Had I considered buying specially tailored blouses that would fit better. Maybe I should have the salad instead of the steak. That I should skip the potatoes because I couldn't afford the carbs. I should exercise more to lose the extra poundage. Not pounds. Poundage. Think before I speak. Finally he just came out and said if I wanted to stay with him I needed to lose weight."

Ian had returned to petting the dog, but the tick in his jawline told her he might be doing that more to soothe himself than the animal.

"I told Brett he needed to lose some of the fat in his brain. That plenty of men liked my curves and I didn't need him. Turns out getting rid of him wasn't that easy. Every time I look in the mirror I wonder if I'm really curvy or just fat. When I order dinner, I think should I skip the steak and have the salad. I know I shouldn't let his digs change how I see myself. I've got hips and I've got boobs and there are women who would kill for both and good men who can love and appreciate me for all of me not just how I look. But something about this jerk has just been so hard to shake off." Kelly dared to look up at Ian. "I'm sorry. I didn't mean to ramble."

"You have nothing to be sorry for."

"I don't even know why I'm telling you all this."

"Maybe because I'm listening."

Goose bumps rose along her arms. Four simple words that may have been the nicest thing any man had ever said to her. Somebody paying attention to what was in her heart not on her chest, and just her luck, he had to be a Farraday. Not just a Farraday who probably saw her as nothing more than a kid sister, but one who wouldn't be around long enough for her to get to know better. And wasn't that just a damn shame?

● ● ● ●

It was a good thing for this Brett character that Ian wasn't in the same room or he might very well have snapped Brett's neck in two like the chicken bone they'd cut out of this little puppy. The guy probably had a brain—and balls—the size of a peanut. There were plenty of things in this life Ian didn't care for. Plenty of things ticked him off. Verbal and emotional abuse was at the top of his list, right after violence and nestled tightly beside animal cruelty.

The way Kelly's eyes widened slightly at his words told him whatever he'd said was either really, really right or really, really wrong, and he had no idea which. Waiting silently for her to say something, do something, to better show him what he'd done, was more unnerving than waiting for the jury's verdict on a case that took years to build.

Puppy broke the silent tension, nudging Ian's now still hand.

"Sorry, boy."

"He needs a name." Kelly's expression shifted from surprise to warmth.

Too bad the warmth was directed at the dog. Not that Ian had the right to be thinking that way. Nor did he have a logical reason for caring. But he did.

"I don't think Rover will cut it." Kelly ran her finger along the puppy's nose.

"Maybe if your name was Jane." He tossed a casual grin in her direction and nearly did a fist pump when she returned the smile.

"He's so cute."

"He is." There was more he wanted to say, but those few words were all that he dared. For now.

"Your Uncle Sean says a good cow dog should have a single syllable name to make commands easier to follow."

Ian nodded. Even when dogs had longer names connecting their breeding, ranchers usually called shorter names. "Planning on giving him away some day?"

Surprised eyes looked up at him again. "No."

"Then you can name him anything you want."

Her head bobbed up and down as though she were not merely answering but convincing herself. "Buddy," she whispered.

"Thinking he might give you a name?"

Kelly smiled up at him again. "You called him Buddy a few times. If it's good enough for a president's dog, why not good enough for him?"

"Why not?" The name suited the dog. Ian felt certain Buddy would be his master's best friend.

"Then Buddy Morgan it is." Reaching for the new dog bed, Kelly slid it under Buddy's head as she pushed to her feet.

He continued stroking Kelly's new dog until she returned with a bowl of freshwater.

"Let's see if he's interested in re-hydrating." Setting the dish near the dog, Kelly stood watching.

At the sound of the metal dish scraping along the floor, the puppy opened his eyes but didn't lift his head. He carefully watched Kelly's movements as she released the bowl and stepped back. For a few seconds Ian thought the dog's groggy gaze seemed to be waiting to see if she'd kneel down and scratch his head once again.

"Not thirsty, Buddy?" Her voice came out soft, low, and coaxing.

Ian didn't know about the dog, but if she'd brought him a glass of water he would've certainly drank his fill. Much like the dog, he kept his eyes on Kelly's every movement as well.

Without moving his head, the dog shifted his gaze from Kelly to the water and back again. Slowly, he lifted his head and shifting his weight, inched closer to the bowl.

Kelly's face lit with delight as the puppy took one and then two quick laps of water.

"You have a beautiful smile." The words slipped from Ian's lips before he could think.

A lovely shade of pink tinged Kelly's cheeks at the same time her mouth fell slightly open before snapping tightly shut. "You don't have to say that."

"No, I don't. I shouldn't have just blurted that out, but it's the truth."

It took her too long to toss back a thank you. This Brett had really done a number on her. He wished he had enough time to convince her he'd meant what he said. That he wasn't being merely polite. Watching her cheeks still tinged with a hint of pink, and the appreciative smile that had taken over her face as she watched the dog drink and nibble on a few treats, he wished he had a hell of a lot more time.

CHAPTER TWELVE

"I know cattle aren't the same as sheep, but something's not right here."

This time he couldn't argue with his brother. None of the other calves stood with their backs humped and their heads down ,and he was pretty sure this one had a runny nose too. They definitely needed a professional. The only problem being they couldn't very well ask any of the ranchers, nor could they waltz into the veterinary clinic with the sick stolen calf and ask for medical attention.

"Do you suppose we need to separate him from the other cows? That whatever has him off is contagious?"

Oh for land's sake how the hell was he supposed to know that? Since they'd begun appropriating calves one by one over the last few months these animals had been pretty maintenance free. Water, grass, a little shade, and they were happy as clams. None of them, especially the ones they'd taken early on, were by any means small or easily transportable. Weaned calves started weighing in at over 400 pounds and this one weighed a hell of a lot more than that.

How the heck were they supposed to move this bad boy away from the other cows and keep him away? Getting cattle to do something they didn't want to do wasn't like offering a treat to a trained seal. Even more importantly, who the heck could they get to take a look at the animal and tell them what kind of treatment he needed without getting them in trouble for having the cattle here in the first place.

"You're doing that thinking thing again. I really do wish you'd think a little less and come up with ideas a little more." His brother looked left then right, scanning the depths of the grazing land before his gaze settled at the foot of the road. "Think we can use that to transport him to the vet?"

"We can't take him to the vet. How are we going to explain having a sick calf?" To boot, one standing in the open for all to see as they drove through town. So not a good idea.

Using one finger, his brother scratched the back of his head. "I suppose you do have a point"

Of course he did. Except he needed more than a point. He needed a plan.

• • • •

Sunday supper at Uncle Sean and Aunt Eileen's was basically the same as supper at Ian's parents only on steroids. With more than twice as many children as his mom and dad had, and all of those children married or almost married, and grandchildren in the mix, the house was almost bursting at the seams.

"Here you go. Set this on the table." Aunt Eileen handed him a bowl of garlic parmesan mashed potatoes.

"Oh, you'll need this." His cousin Adam's wife Meg shoved a large serving spoon into the bowl.

"Oh," his cousin Connor's wife Catherine shoved a handful of napkins at his chest, "take these too, please."

"Sure." Ian nodded, pressing the napkins between his chin and chest.

Beside him his cousin DJ appeared with a salad bowl the size of a small watering tub for cattle. "Just got off the phone with Esther. Sheriff next county over called. Rancher's sons were camping out near a pasture and called him about seeing a strange truck. Rancher got there as they were done loading up."

"They've got them?"

"One of them. Last guy didn't make it into the truck before the rancher pointed a double barrel at his face."

Ian chuckled softly and set the bowl on the table, stepping back out of the crowd of relatives scurrying about with food and silverware and drinks, laughing and chatting and teasing as they squeezed by. He was Texas born and bred where guns were sacred. Some days he really hated what guns did when they fell into the wrong hands, but he'd take a sharp shooting rancher having his back any day of the week, and like now, twice on Sundays. "Think they're our guys?"

"Hard to tell yet." DJ shifted to one side out of the traffic flow.

"Oh dang!" a female voice cried from the kitchen, smothered in a crashing sound.

Another voice shouted, "Cold water" while another called, "I'll get the ice."

Allison, the other doctor in the family, slammed a gravy boat on the table, spun in place and now holding her baby niece firmly in two hands, shoved her at Ian. "I need to see what the heck just happened."

This Uncle Ian thing was new to him, and clearly the rest of the Uncles must have been better trained because Allison turned around and tore off toward the kitchen with complete confidence that Ian had a firm grip on his niece Brittany. Only his ranger reflexes had him quickly recovering from the five second bobble that, thank heaven, his niece thought was a fun game and giggled.

Holding her high up in the air and swishing her left and right like a tiny airplane, he kept his eye on her sweet smiles. "Yet?"

DJ shrugged. "They had a large truck."

"That could fit." Ian got a bit more brazen and tossed Brittany a couple of inches higher, grinning almost as wide as his niece.

"Yeah, but the truck was loaded with grown cattle ready for market."

Ian sighed and shifted to swirling Brittany at arms length, left than right. "Could be they're done practicing and upgrading to the real plan."

"Thought crossed my mind." DJ got in on the fun and pretended to grab for Brittany's nose every time she came near him. "Sheriff's going to get back with me after he's got some more info from the guy."

"If he gets more info from him."

"Probably will. Says the guy's pretty young and scared at being caught. Right now he's sitting in a cell getting more scared by the minute."

"That'll work if he doesn't lawyer up." Now Ian was shoving Brittany up in the air and pulling her down to blow air on her tummy. "This baby thing is pretty fun."

DJ laughed and nodded. "Especially for us uncles who are spared diaper duty."

"Okay." Allison reappeared and Brittany threw herself at the woman who was raising her. Hefting the little girl onto one hip, Allison looked up at the two men. "Grace dropped the baked sweet potatoes on the floor and they splashed on her foot and hand. Doesn't matter what it is, heated to over 200 degrees anything will burn."

DJ looked over her shoulder into the kitchen. "She okay?"

"Yeah. The ladies had it covered. Stuck her hand under the faucet and put ice on the foot."

"Guess it would have been hard shoving the foot under the faucet." Still enchanted with his niece, Ian continued to play with her, poking his finger at her tummy.

Allison swallowed a laugh. "Honestly, I wouldn't have put it past them to lift her up and stuff her in the sink if they had to."

The last of the hot food out, the remainder of the family gathered around the table. Allison walked away to place Brittany in her high chair and Ian followed behind, understanding at least a little better why his friends practically glowed when they had children. For the first time he felt like by not dating seriously, not having a family plan on his radar, he might be missing out on more than he'd admitted.

Taking his seat, he looked at the smiling faces, the couples holding hands, the love and adoration in respectful gazes and wondered how Kelly was holding up alone with her grandfather and great uncle. Maybe after supper he'd pop over. After all, he had every good reason to check up on Buddy. And maybe if he could keep a straight face she'd believe that when he showed up later on her doorstep.

• • • •

"I forgot how much I enjoy the beach." Kelly's mom sighed into the phone. Houston was only a short drive to the Galveston coast. "There's nothing that compares with the sand between your toes, the gulls squawking as they swoop in and out of the water, and the setting sun sparkling on the waves."

"I'm glad you're having a good time. You coming home today?"

"Well…" the lagging silence said more than if her mom had spoken. "Marilyn has to go to Charleston next."

Even before her mother finished the last syllable, Kelly knew what was coming. Her mom was off for an extended adventure and Kelly would be in charge of her grandfather for a little longer. "How long?"

"Just a week."

"A week?"

"Is that too long? Is Pops giving you trouble? If they've gotten into more—"

"No. They're fine." Actually, they'd been rather easy maintenance. During the day they'd gone into town to play cards with friends, and had kept their promise to stay away from cooking until she got home. Maybe she'd been stressing over nothing and another week wouldn't be a problem. She resisted the urge to sing liar, liar pants on fire. She was only kidding herself. Every evening she came home praying she wouldn't find her grandfather in the midst of chaos or the house in ashes, but good, bad, or ugly, one more week wasn't going to kill her. "You deserve a nice vacation. Enjoy hanging out with Marilyn."

Five days post surgery, Buddy had way more energy than was probably good for him. He'd trotted to the kitchen door and back to Kelly a couple of times since she sat to chat with her mom. Now his tail was wagging a mile a minute and he was furtively bouncing from door to table and back.

"What about you, dear? Anything interesting happening?"

Interesting was her mother's code for new man in her life. Kelly hadn't seen the need to tell her mother that she'd sworn off men at least for now. And she sure as heck wasn't going to mention the only man to spark her interest since kicking Brett to the door months ago was a Farraday. "Just working hard."

"And the puppy?"

The little guy was now spinning in circles by the back door. Kelly really wished she could just open the door and let him out to run, but Adam had said no serious exercise for at least a week. So, Buddy had been confined to short walks up and down the block on a leash. "Just a few more days, fella."

"Excuse me?"

"Not you, Mom. The dog. He's just champing at the bit to get out into the yard and run around. Probably wants to chase the chickens."

"Or herd them." Her mom laughed. "How's Pops getting along with him?"

"How does Peanut Butter like Jelly?"

"Thought so. It'll be good for him to have a new project."

"Yeah. This will probably be the best thing…" A flash of red and white caught the corner of her eye. They didn't have any red chickens. Pushing away from the table she crossed the room and stood by the window, then blinked twice before she believed her eyes. "Holy mother of …. Mom, you go have fun. I need to take care of a few things here."

She didn't even wait for her mother to say goodbye before tossing her phone onto the counter and taking another look out the window, just in case she was hallucinating. No such luck. *So much for Pops staying out of trouble.*

CHAPTER THIRTEEN

"Will you slow down!" Herbert shouted to his brother.

"It's a bloody golf cart," Ralph called over his shoulder. "How fast do you think I can go?"

"Faster than the cow. Slow down."

"I thought the idea was to get him in the garage as fast as we can so the neighbors don't see him."

"Yeah, but if the animal drops from exhaustion or disease first, he's going to be hard as hell to hide. Take it easy." Herbert and his brother had spent the better part of the morning dealing with isolating the sick calf. Once they'd stopped arguing with each other as to whether or not the calf was contagious, and after they'd agreed it was best to keep him closer to home, the next debate had been how to accomplish moving him.

They'd already mastered putting them in a head catch to get halters on them, so that part of the day had gone well enough, but this time they hadn't rented a truck. Besides, on a Sunday renting any car within reasonable driving distance was not an option.

Ralph sputtered to a halt.

"Why'd you stop?"

"Ask the cow."

"What?" Herbert had been following at the rear of the calf for the last hour. They'd come the back way, far enough behind all the development of the town so that no one would see them. The biggest risk had been coming in the short distance to the backyard.

"I'm stepping on the gas but I'm not going anywhere. Ask junior back there what happened." Herbert carefully circled the animal, giving it a wide berth to avoid being accidentally kicked or stomped. "Come on. Time to get going." Herbert tsked at the animal the way he would a horse. Big cow eyes looked up at him. "Don't give me that dirty look. We got a few more feet to go to the garage. Let's move it." Herbert slapped the calf's rump the way he might do to a horse. The problem at hand was that a horse would gallop off, this animal just kept staring at him.

"Well?" Ralph asked.

"Well nothing. He doesn't want to move."

"Where did you put that red sweater?"

Herbert refrained from rolling his eyes and praying to the heavens for a miraculously more astute brother. "I left it in the car. It isn't going to help any more now than it did back at the golf course. Waving your sweater in the cow's face isn't gonna make him move. He's not a grown bull and this is not Pamplona."

"Pam who?"

This time Herbert looked up to the sky, sucked in a deep breath, and turned to the cow, lowering his voice. "It's only a few more feet. Couldn't you just move forward for me?"

He'd swear on his ancestors' grave the cow smacked his lips and shook his head. Then again maybe he'd simply spent too much time in the sun.

• • • •

Kelly couldn't run fast enough. As much as she'd love to believe she was hallucinating, as clear as the nose on her face, strolling across the backyard like a rat after the Pied Piper was Pops, following behind Uncle Ralph riding a golf cart with a cow tied to the back end.

"Oh dear Lord," she practically screeched as she bolted from the house, the screen door slamming shut behind her. Buddy came happily prancing after her and Kelly didn't take the time to stop him. Her grandfather was now hovering over the stocky animal. What the hell was he doing with a cow? Weren't the colorful assortment of chickens they kept enough of a menagerie?

The startled look on her grandfather's face at the sight of her quickly shifted to calm and relaxed. The man straightened in place and stared at her with a bright smile as though hanging around the backyard with a cow was a perfectly normal thing for them. "Kelly dear, we thought you were going to be having Sunday supper with Becky and Grace at the Farraday's."

"I didn't want to leave Buddy." Truthfully, she didn't want to leave her grandfather and clearly she'd been right. Now she stood at a complete loss for what to say next. Well, except for the obvious. "Why is there a cow in our backyard?"

"Oh," her grandfather cast a furtive glance at his brother, then the cow, and then back to her, "well, um, he ah…"

"Is feeling poorly," Uncle Ralph said.

The cow appeared rooted in place with a runny nose. "I can see that."

"You know something about sick cows?" Her grandfather's face lit with interest.

Years working with Adam she'd learned enough about dogs, cats, *and* cows, to occasionally be helpful, though in this case, any moron could tell the cow's nose was runny.

"We got him this far," Pops said, "and now he won't move."

Stepping close enough to the animal to grab its tail and twist it, Kelly gave a small shove. Usually that would be enough to make a cow move, but if the animal doesn't feel well, getting it to budge even a little could prove to be a battle of wills. "Whose cow is it, and where are you taking it?"

"Um," her Pops muttered again. "A… uh…friend of ours is getting into the er… cattle business…"

"Yes," Uncle Ralph nodded with a bit more enthusiasm than the response warranted. "That's it. A friend, and he wanted to separate this calf from the rest of the herd until he could get to a vet—"

"Right," Pops smiled, "and we suggested he keep it in our garage until then." The grin on her grandfather's face broadened to the point that anyone watching would think he'd just been nominated for a Nobel prize.

Something simply did not make sense. She only hoped her grandfather hadn't gone and bought a damn cow with some crazy notion of starting a cattle business and now planned to hide a herd in their two-car garage. Shaking her head, she stepped back. "Let me go inside and get an empty water bottle. At the Farradays I've seen them shake a plastic bottle filled with rocks at a cow. Sick or healthy that always seemed to make them move. I'll be right back."

Front end low to the ground, butt in the air, surgical cone dragging on the ground, Buddy kept careful watch on the lone cow.

"Come on, Buddy." Kelly snapped her fingers low to her side. "Come with me."

The puppy jerked his head left then right, looking to her, then the cow and back before finally following orders and prancing up to her side.

"Good boy." She patted the top of his head and gave an extra scratch behind his ear. At least one member of this family was staying out of trouble.

Finding a small plastic bottle in the kitchen to use was easy, the pebbles to shake was another story. The idea of substituting pennies occurred to her, but she wasn't sure if it would have the same affect. Empty bottle in hand, she stepped outside making sure Buddy didn't follow and pulled the back door shut behind her at the same moment her cell phone went off. Her heart did a little dance when she recognized the number as Ian's.

The other night at the clinic the two of them had stayed for hours sitting with Buddy, talking, and visiting as though they had been close friends for years. By the time the tech had finally arrived, he'd griped and grumbled and mumbled so often about what a loser, idiot, and all around jerk Brett was for letting her go, and how he didn't deserve her, for the first time in months Ian actually had her believing the problem really was Brett. Her head had known that all along, but her heart had been slow to get with the program. Not a single day this week had she looked in the mirror and had second thoughts about anything.

It hadn't hurt any that Ian had come to town Friday afternoon to pick up some supplies at the feed store and invited her dancing at the Boots and Scoots. She had so wanted to say yes, but with her mom away, she wasn't comfortable leaving the old men alone at home for too long. She had however agreed to a rain check, and seriously hoped he would take her up on it.

"Hello." She sucked in a calming breath and crossed the yard to her grandfather.

"Hi," Ian said lightly. "Thought you might be joining us for supper today."

"No. I hope Becky explained why I couldn't go to Aunt Eileen."

"She did. Which is why I come bearing leftovers from my aunt. Enough to feed all your distant relatives for a fortnight."

Kelly giggled. She should have expected as much.

"I'm turning the corner now."

"Now?" Not that she didn't want to see him, but she didn't want to explain a cow in the yard. Ian already knew about the fence, the chickens, and the fire, she wasn't up to pretending a grandfather bringing a cow home was normal.

"Is that a problem?"

"No. Not at all."

"Good. See you in a minute."

The call disconnected and she slid the phone into her pocket and hurried the last few steps up to the cow and her grandpa. "We've only got a few minutes." *Hiccup.* "Uncle Ralph, you move the golf cart into the garage." She turned back to her grandfather. "You gather some pebbles from the footpath, load them into the bottle, then shake them behind the cow. That should get it to move."

Both men nodded. Her grandfather scurried off to the path, Uncle Ralph untied the cow from the cart, and she debated between helping her grandfather and taking a minute inside to at least put on some blush or lipstick, but she didn't have time for either when she heard the short loud beep signaling Ian had arrived and locked his truck. He must have literally been halfway up the street when he called her.

"I have to go inside," she shouted to her grandfather, a little more frantically than she'd intended. "Please hurry. I don't want Ian to see the cow." *Hiccup.*

"Ian Farraday is calling on you?" Her grandfather stopped in his tracks and turned to look at her.

"The rocks," she yelled over her shoulder, already hurrying toward the house, "the cow. And put away that cart!" There was no way she was going to discuss Ian Farraday now, she just wanted the cow out of sight.

She'd made it to the kitchen door in time to hear the front bell ring and see her grandfather grudgingly returning to his task of gathering stones. Uncle Ralph had the cart parked inside the garage and was pulling the door down to hide the evidence, but the cow still stood in place, back slightly hunched, head down, and she prayed they moved the poor thing before he plopped on the ground where he stood and took a much needed nap.

Buddy beat her to the door, tail wagging and making noises that sounded more like a conversation than a bark.

"Hang on," she told the puppy, took a deep calming, and hopefully hiccup smothering breath, and swung the door open wide.

Standing with a shopping bag in each hand, Ian stretched them out in front of her. "In the kitchen?"

"Oh, uh." That was the last place she wanted him with a birds eye view of the circus in her yard. "Let me."

"I can take them."

"That won't be necessary, uh," she sucked in another breath before a hiccup escaped. "Buddy here is going to jump out of his skin if he doesn't get some one on one ear scratching from his rescuer."

For all of two seconds she thought he was going to object, but instead Buddy, bless him, tail still swishing frantically back and forth, pawed anxiously at Ian, bringing a smile to the man's face. "Okay, boy." He nodded at Kelly, handing over the two bags before squatting to scratch the puppy.

Glancing quickly at each one, Kelly spun around, and hurrying to the kitchen, called back to Ian. "You weren't kidding. Aunt Eileen must think I'm feeding an army."

"You know how she is."

"Yeah," Kelly chuckled, "I do." Placing the bags on the table, she sneaked a peek out the kitchen window, relieved to at least see the golf cart was gone. So startled at the sight of a cow, only now did she stop to wonder what the heck they were doing with a golf cart. And that would have to be a concern for another time.

Puppy nails clacked against the wooden floor. The sound growing closer tripped Kelly's heart rate into double time and a soft hiccup escaped. Before she could work her way around the table, Ian and Buddy were standing in the doorway.

"He's doing really well."

"Yes. Yes, he is." She maneuvered quickly around the table and placed herself between Ian and a view of the window. Not that it would do much good, with him being a head taller than her. "Let's have a seat in the other room."

Not in line with the plan, Buddy slipped past Kelly making a beeline for the back door.

"Buddy." Kelly shifted again snapping her fingers at the dog. "Come here, Buddy. Come on."

"Looks like he wants to go outside."

"Yes well, he's not allowed to run around for at least a couple more days. You go on and sit down inside, I'll bring him along." Placing her hand on Ian's arm she gently nudged him away from the kitchen, but the man was built like a stone statue. It would take much more than a gentle nudge to move a Farraday.

"If he's that anxious to go out maybe we can keep an eye on him."

"Better safe than sorry." Kelly smiled up and considered another nudge when Ian turned toward the bank of rear windows and she swallowed another hiccup.

"And look." He pointed to the first corner window. "Here comes your grandfather."

Two more windows and he'd be staring straight at the cow.

"He loves being outside. Why don't we go into the living room?"

Ian shifted another few inches to his right and Kelly knew any second he'd see the cow.

Mortification laced with panic seized her. She had to make him move. Throwing one arm up by his shoulder and splaying her other hand, palm open across his chest, she pushed up on her toes ready to shove a little harder when his startled gaze latched onto hers. Suddenly the room seemed to shrink around her. The thwacking of Buddy's tail against the floor and his paw scratching at the door faded into silence. Fear of her grandfather and the mysterious cow coming into view melted away.

She needed to move him forward or step back, but all she could do was stare at the most beautiful sea green eyes she'd ever seen.

"Kelly," he murmured softly. His fingers curled around her arms. Whether hanging on or holding her steady, she wasn't sure and didn't care. Standing a breath apart, there was only one thing she knew. Ian Farraday was about to kiss her and she wasn't going to do a damn thing to stop him.

CHAPTER FOURTEEN

When Kelly placed her one hand on his shoulder, Ian had no idea what she intended. By the time her second hand landed squarely on his chest he was more than confused. Not till her eyes locked on his did he not give a flip what she was doing. The only thing he could think of was pulling her into his arms and tasting those rosy pink lips.

He wanted to say something. Words hardly ever failed him, but now, the only thing he'd managed to mumble was her name. Drawing on every ounce of honor and chivalry his family had drummed into him, he waited, searching her eyes, wanting to be absolutely sure the electricity heightening his senses wasn't one sided.

Afraid to let go of her, and even more afraid to let his hands fall to those well-rounded hips, he dared to inch closer. Leaving her time and space to step away, to say no. Bracing himself for a slap in the face if he'd misread the look she gave him, close enough to count the golden flecks in her eyes, he lowered his mouth to hers for the barest of caresses, softly repeating her name one more time before letting his lips meet hers.

"What in blue blazes?" Brows buckled with irritation, Kelly's grandfather stood anchored by the back door until his brother slammed into him, shoving him two feet forward and closing the door behind him.

Kelly sprang out of Ian's grasp in a single leap. Not since Ian had been sixteen and caught making out with Natalie Franks at her pool house by Natalie's grandmother had he felt so completely embarrassed. Apparently neither being a full grown legal adult, nor barely getting a touch of Kelly's soft lips, made getting caught any less awkward.

"Pops." Kelly stepped around the table and busied herself unloading the bags of leftovers. "Did you get everything put away?"

"Pretty much." Kelly's grandfather crossed the room and turned on the kitchen sink to wash his hands, his brother a step behind him.

Ian had no idea what *everything* entailed, but her grandfather's demeanor had shifted on a dime from scowling protector to contrite subordinate. Wasn't that as much of a surprise as getting caught too close to a woman who by most people's standards he barely knew, and yet somehow he felt like he didn't know anyone better than he knew her. "Anything I can help with?" He figured volunteering might go a long way to getting him out of the doghouse with Kelly's grandfather.

"No," three voices barked.

Again, not the reaction he'd expected.

Drying his hand on the dishtowel, her grandfather stared out the window as though searching for something before turning around to face them. "I'm heading up to my room. It's been a busy day and I'm ready for a nice, hot shower."

"I'll second that," Ralph chorused.

Kelly's grandfather paused in front of Ian. "You remember, I'm just up the stairs."

"Yes, sir," Ian nodded. He and Kelly were certainly old enough to kiss. Technically they were well above the age of consent for a lot of things, but Ian had been raised, like his cousins, with an old-fashioned set of standards. A standard as common in small town USA as mom's apple pie and the American flag.

Neither he nor Kelly moved a muscle until her grandfather and great uncle were down the hall and halfway up the stairs. The air in the room was thick and tense and he was pretty sure it had little to do with his impromptu attempt at a kiss. Turning to face her and taking a long stride in her direction, Ian stopped where Buddy sat midway between them. "There's more going on here than just a kiss, isn't there?"

Kelly resumed her task of putting away the leftovers. "I'm not sure what you mean."

"Neither do I, but something seems off." He gave Buddy a quick pat on the head and closed the distance between him and Kelly. "Are you okay?"

Her hands stilled from unpacking. She took in a long breath and nodded. "I will be."

"Your grandfather is giving you more trouble?"

"Nothing I can't handle."

"Anything I can help with?"

Her head turned from side to side. "Nothing I can't handle," she repeated.

"Would you tell me if it *were* something you couldn't handle?"

"Of course…" Her words stilled a moment, her head tipped slightly to one side and her gaze shifted from casual to intense, and then with the slightest of smiles, she nodded. "Yes, I think I would."

He couldn't help but smile back. In little more than a week they'd developed a sincere camaraderie and he liked it. A lot. "I'd better be on my way before I do something your grandfather will really get mad at me for."

With that, he gave her a quick peck on the temple before the temptation to aim for her mouth took over his good sense.

Kelly accompanied him to the front door. "Please tell Aunt Eileen I said thank you."

"I will."

At the door she pulled it open and stood almost barricaded behind it. He hoped he hadn't made a mistake kissing her. But if he had, he hoped he'd get a better chance to do it again.

• • • •

Regardless of having finished putting away the leftovers, tidied up the kitchen, and played with the dog, Kelly couldn't stop thinking of the cow her grandfather had brought home, but couldn't bring herself to go outside and look at it. She'd tried the out of sight out of mind thing, but it wasn't working for her. Finally running out of things to do, she was about to head out to the garage when her grandfather came downstairs.

As was his routine late every evening, he poked his head in the fridge looking for a snack most people would call a meal. Except this time he didn't say anything to her. As a matter of fact, she got the feeling he'd intentionally talked to the dog on his way to the fridge to avoid facing her.

"Pops. We need to talk."

"I was thinking the same thing." He emerged from looking into the fridge with a large pan of Aunt Eileen's leftovers. "You're a pretty sensible girl."

"I'd like to think so." At least she knew she was sensible enough not to bring a five hundred pound calf home for some TLC.

Pops peeled the foil back from the tray, reached behind him for a dish, and holding a large spoon, scooped a mound onto the plate. She must have inherited her metabolism from him. As full figured as she was, she'd never been as heavy as she should be based on the amount of food she could eat.

By the time Pops had dawdled and stalled by adding corn on the cob and green bean casserole to the already full plate, irritation mingled with impatience had Kelly nearly tapping her toe. "Pops."

He held a finger up to her, slid the plate into the microwave and turning around, pinned her with a sharp steely look that almost made her take a step back. "I like the Farradays."

That hadn't been the opening she'd been expecting.

"I like them a lot. Good, honest, hardworking people. Even if they do raise helpless animals for food—"

"I'm in no mood for a lecture on the benefits of a vegetarian diet."

He bobbed his head. "And this isn't the time to give one. You know Ian Farraday is a grown man."

Surely her grandfather didn't think she was stupid *and* blind.

"A man doesn't make it to his age and stay a bachelor without having enjoyed a few oats along the way."

Oats?

"You're still pretty young and I know most women find the Farradays easy on the eyes. Ian is no exception, but I don't want those boyish good looks fooling you. Ian Farraday is going back to his life and world as soon as Finn and his bride come home—"

"Pops—"

"Don't Pops me." He pulled the dish out of the beeping microwave and pinned her with another serious glare. "I've seen the pretty little things men like that dally with. Even if he is a Farraday, he's still a man and you're not that type."

"Pops." An unexpected ache pinched in her chest. Whether it was hearing the words straight out that nothing could come from a relationship, okay maybe not a relationship but at least another kiss, or two, or more with Ian, or the implication that she wasn't pretty enough for a Farraday that stabbed at her, she wasn't sure, but her grandfather's words stung nonetheless. Sadly, both were probably true. All the Farraday wives were varying types of striking and attractive women, and all were smart as whips. Hell, Allison was a world famous doctor and Catherine had run legal circles around some of the best lawyers in the Midwest.

Pops came around to her side, a softer gleam in his gaze. "You'll find the right man, one who appreciates and loves you for the amazing beautiful person you are, but don't be thinking that's Ian Farraday."

Understanding her grandfather's intent more clearly, she hated to admit that as interesting, in a whole lot of ways, that getting to know Ian Farraday a whole lot better, held a whole lot of appeal, her grandfather was right. She needed to remember this wasn't about her being good enough or pretty enough, and about Ian not sticking around long enough.

But even more critical at this very moment, the real issue at hand she needed to deal with now wasn't her love life or lack of one, but her grandfather and his crazy cow ideas. She gave her grandfather a quick peck on the cheek. "Thanks for worrying, Pop, but there's nothing going on with me and Ian. I was just trying to distract him from looking out the window and spotting you and Uncle Ralph with the cow."

At least her grandfather had the good sense to look a tad repentant. Whether about the cow itself, or her finding it, she couldn't tell.

"Which brings me back to the real problem. The cow."

Pops bristled before stabbing at his mashed potatoes. "You don't need to worry yourself about that. Ralph and… my friend and I will handle it."

"That's what worries me." She turned away heading for the back door. Someone had to be the sensible one around here and it appeared she was the one with the most experience around animals and illness. "Why would any rancher give two greenhorns a sick cow to care for?"

She was halfway out the door when her grandfather tossed his fork down and hurried after her. "We know what we're doing. No need to go after the calf."

Kelly continued the short distance to the garage. Like it or not her grandfather had proven one time too many that she couldn't rely on him to handle much of anything anymore and in this case there was a sick cow on her property. She'd probably need to call in Adam, but at least she could get a better look at what the animal's symptoms were before she called her boss.

"Now, young lady, you're not so grown up that you don't have to listen to your grandpa any more," he said more sternly as she reached for the handle on the side door to the garage. "Let's go back to the house and let me and Ralph handle this."

"Pops, I can't do that. We probably need to call Adam over before it gets any later." Kelly walked all of two paces before coming up to the rear end of a growing beef cow standing in an empty garage. No hay, no water, no barriers to keep him out of things he shouldn't get into. She shook her head. What a bloody mess.

Taking another step closer, her grandfather scurried around her intent on blocking her path, but not before the sliver of light from the doorway shone on the cow's rump and a bold print F inside a circle. The Farraday brand. A Farraday cow. A sick Farraday cow.

Her head snapped left to her grandfather's crestfallen face. "Oh, Pops. What on earth have you done now?"

CHAPTER FIFTEEN

Already blocks from Kelly's house, Ian's head was still reeling from the last few minutes. The slightest of kisses had left an impact on him he couldn't shake. None of which made any sense. The entire interaction barely qualified as a real kiss, and yet, it had affected him more than any other kiss before.

Turning the corner onto Main Street, he considered what to do. He only had another week until he had to report back to work, and most of that time would be spent more than an hour out of town at the ranch, all of which made spending time with Kelly difficult, but right now spending time with Kelly was something he really wanted to do. Needed to do. Another thing that made no sense. He'd met lots of women in his years. Liked lots of women. A time or two he'd been so infatuated he'd thought he might have found the right one, but time always wore away the illusion and settled into nice girls to date, but nothing he couldn't shake. Until Kelly, and that scared him clear to the marrow of his bones.

Coming up near the Cut and Curl, Ian slowed at what he thought was the sight of his brother's beat up old pick up. Though it was very unlikely Jamison would come to town and no one in the family know about it, it was even less likely there were two of that old truck in this world. Sure enough, slowing to a near crawl for a better look, not only was it Jamison's truck he'd spotted parked to the side, but his brother stood on the sidewalk grinning up at the building in front of him.

Apparently he wasn't the only one surprised to find Jamison in town. Walking at a brisk pace, Sissy waved frantically while Sister locked the door to their boutique. And wasn't that an odd sight. Not that there was anything odd about the sisters chasing down the street after anyone, more that they were coming from their store at this hour. Unlike the rest of the modern world, the shops on Main Street were all closed on Sundays. Sisters was no exception.

By the time he'd parked and climbed out of the truck, both sisters were deep in animated conversation with his brother. Jamison, bless his heart, was smiling, and nodding, and laying on all the Farraday charm at his disposal and the sisters were grinning back like a couple of giddy school girls. Lord, how Ian loved this town.

"Am I invited to this party?" Ian called from the curb, slapping his brother on the shoulder and pulling him into a hug once he reached his side. "Does Aunt Eileen know you're coming?"

"Until a few hours ago, I didn't know I was coming."

"Jamison was just telling us the good news." Sissy, the taller of the two sisters, said.

"Yes," Sister, who after all these years still wore her hair as high as it was wide keeping the idea of Texas big hair alive and well, said, "He may be moving to Tuckers Bluff."

"Really?" Ian's brother had been somewhat cryptic about an upcoming project for some time. The last time they'd had a chance to sit down and really talk, Jamie had implied a sweet deal was coming together. Ian couldn't believe the deal was in Farraday country.

"Still a few dots and tiddles to work out, but it's looking really good."

"Well," Sissy looked to her sister, "we should be getting home. Only came to the store cause Sister thought she'd left the iron plugged in and turned on."

"Silly me," Sister rolled her eyes. "Of course I hadn't, but I wouldn't have gotten a wink of sleep tonight second guessing myself."

Sissy nodded. "Keep us posted, Jamie."

"I will." He waved at the two women as they waddled up the

road toward their house.

"Moving to town?" Ian repeated.

Jamison tilted his head toward the building behind them. "If we can get old man Thomas to sell this building."

"What in the name of…" DJ stepped out of his police car. "I thought it was you jawing with Ian. What are you doing in town and is Aunt Eileen expecting you?"

"Looking around, and no, I thought I'd surprise her."

"Well, that you will, and she'll like having you," DJ smiled, "but she won't like not being ready with some special treat."

Jamie's grin grew to match DJ's. "I may have to stick around long enough for her to bake something."

"You do that." DJ lifted his chin pointing at his cousin. "So what exactly are you looking around at? You've only been to town a million times?"

"This building." Jamie threw his thumb over his shoulder. "Meeting with old man Thomas tomorrow morning.

"What about?" DJ asked what Ian was thinking.

The smile on Jamie's face grew impossibly wider. "I wasn't at liberty to say anything before, and this is still just between us, but if the price is right, there's going to be a new pub in town."

"Son of a…" DJ whistled. "Mabel was right."

"Right?" Jamie asked.

"A referendum to make Tuckers Bluff wet."

Jamie nodded. "Yep. There's been a county wide move and Tuckers Bluff is smack dab in the middle of it."

"But a pub?" Ian asked. "Do you really think this town is big enough to support it?"

"Not just this town, this county. Folks won't have to drive all the way to Butler Springs for a Saturday night date or some Friday night two stepping."

"Well," DJ shrugged, "that might be true for Friday and Saturday, but what do you do the rest of the week?"

"Only going to be open Thursday through Sunday."

Ian lifted a brow. "Four day work week?"

"The demographic studies say it will work. I'll make it work." Jamie shot his brother the same confident look he'd given his dad when he'd announced he'd had enough of college and was going to find his own way.

Ian knew his brother had done well for himself, but didn't realize he'd done that well. Come to think of it. "Where'd you come up with enough money to buy a building?"

"It's a partnership." For a flashing moment, the light in Jamie's eyes appeared to dim before enthusiasm took over again. Looking from DJ to Ian, Jamie paused. "Speaking of unexpected encounters, I'm not surprised to run into DJ here in town, but what are you doing here?"

"Yeah," DJ grinned like the dog who had caught the cat with the canary. "What brought you to town?"

"Me?" Ian repeated innocently.

"Go ahead," DJ coaxed. "Tell him."

Because I didn't want to wait any longer to see Kelly didn't seem like the smartest answer he could give—even if it was the truth—Ian went with the secondary excuse. "I brought some leftovers into town from Aunt Eileen."

Jamie's brows shot up high and DJ chuckled.

"Yeah, we all thought he volunteered a little too fast." DJ looked to Ian. "Tell him who the leftovers were for."

This time Jamie's face lit up. "Tell me there's a girl involved?"

"Yeah, cuz," DJ teased. "Tell him."

If he'd thought he'd kept his thoughts about Kelly quiet, he'd obviously been dead wrong. "Don't you have some new info on the rustlers to share?"

"No. Haven't heard from the sheriff yet." DJ turned to Jamie. "It's Kelly Morgan."

Jamie squinted in thought. "Grace's friend? The pudgy one who works for Adam?"

"She's not pudgy," Ian shot back instantly.

Jamie's brows shot up high on his forehead once again.

"Really?"

"Yes," Ian said more firmly. "Really." He'd be the first to agree as a young child she was indeed a bit on the pudgy side, but now there wasn't anything about Kelly that would be described as pudgy. Words like luscious and shapely came to mind. He'd told her she was beautiful and he wasn't being nice because of the stupid comments her jerk of an ex had said. He'd meant every one of the things he'd said to her.

"Told you," DJ crossed his arms and grinned in Jamie's direction.

"Well, I'll be." Jamie shook his head. "Looks like I'm not the only one with a few surprises up their sleeves."

"What the hell are you talking about?" Ian snapped, still annoyed at the way his brother had described Kelly. People were more than their weight.

"You, my dear brother, are smitten."

Ian didn't know which subject to broach first, the fact that no one used words like smitten any more, or the fact that his brother had to be totally off his rocker to think driving an hour to town to deliver leftovers said anything more than he was a good neighbor to a nice woman. The only problem with that was he knew better than anyone, he was a hell of a lot more than smitten with Kelly. What he didn't know was what the hell was he going to do about it?

• • • •

Kelly stared at the familiar Farraday brand. She knew darn well there was no way any Farraday would give her grandfather a sick cow to tend to. Her mind instantly flashed back to the talk of cattle rustlers. What she couldn't figure out is why her grandfather would help a rustler. Unless of course Pops didn't know the friend was stealing cattle, but who could Pops possibly know who would do such a thing?

"Pops, I don't know who your friend is, or what he told you, but this is a stolen calf, and we have got to get him back to his rightful owners."

"I don't think that's a good idea." The older man shook his head.

"I know you think this person is a friend, and I admire your sense of loyalty to him, but we can't be caught aiding and abetting or whatever it's called when you help hide stolen goods." Not to mention the inside of their garage, with no straw for the flooring or hay and water for the animal, was no place to offer safe harbor.

Uncle Ralph came walking through the door, cast a fast glance at the cow, his brother, and Kelly's hand near the Farraday brand before his eyes widened like a couple of full moons and muttered, "Uh oh."

From the corner of her eye she noticed her grandfather take a half step back and shake his head vehemently at her uncle. Before she could ask what was going on, her uncle ran his hand across the back of his neck. "Well, I guess the jig is up."

Pops' eyes widened twice their normal size. "Ralph, go on back to the house."

"Why? Surely she's not going to turn us in," Uncle Ralph said. "The idea was a good one at first."

"Ralph." Pops stepped forward, nudging his brother toward the door. "You go on and let me and Kelly talk alone."

His back to Kelly, Uncle Ralph moved forward, still talking over his shoulder at her grandfather. "Make sure you explain we thought we was giving them a better life. Never gave no never mind that there's no place to send grown cows."

It took a few seconds for the word *we* to process and register in her mind. Not he or they, but we, as in Ralph and Herbert. "You stole the cows?"

Pops and Uncle Ralph stopped short, both looking so contrite she instantly gave up any hope of being told otherwise. "You stole the cows," she muttered again, only this time it wasn't a question. Her gaze shifted from the two men staring at her in anticipation of her next words, the sickly cow, the golf cart that struck her as being as out of place in her garage as the cow, and thoughts of the man who had just left her kitchen. Her head began to spin. The difference between right and wrong had been drummed into her head since before she could speak. She knew the right thing to do. What she didn't know was how was she supposed to call the police on her own grandfather?

CHAPTER SIXTEEN

"**O**h, by the way," DJ let his crossed arms fall to his side, and the teasing expression gave way to a more serious face, "Esther reported an interesting call a short while ago. I was just on my way to check it out. Since you're here, you might want to come with me."

"On the rustling or something else?" Ian asked.

"Well, that is to be determined. Edna Perkins called in that she saw a golf cart pulling a cow."

"A golf cart?" Ian had heard a lot of strange things in his line of work, and he wasn't ready to discount anything until he'd investigated it fully, but he had to admit a golf cart and a cow didn't sound like a break in the case, more like bad eyesight.

"Miss Edna is pushing 95 years old, has been known to get a little confused from time to time, but considering her age she's usually sharp as a tack."

"A golf cart and a cow," Ian repeated, a hint of incredulity in his voice.

DJ blew out a small sigh and nodded. "I know, but I have to check it out. Do you want to come?"

Something about a golf cart tickled the back of Ian's mind. "Where does this Edna Perkins live?"

"Just outside the south end of town. Houses are pretty scattered out there. Large lots—"

"Near Kelly's family?"

"A little further out. Almost to the old golf club."

Pulling up to Kelly's house earlier, Ian had thought he'd heard a commotion in the yard. Instinctively he'd glanced up the drive and thought he'd noticed someone pulling a riding vehicle into the detached garage. With the size of the lots, a riding mower was not an unusual thing to find. He'd filed the machinery away as just that. Except, now that he thought about it a little more, the thing did have an awning or some sort of covering, and he remembered a flash of color. "What color was the cart?"

"Red and white. Fits the old golf club colors," DJ answered. "Why?"

He'd been so focused on getting to see Kelly when he'd arrived at her house, he hadn't paid much attention to anything else, but now that the scene replayed in his mind, more details stood out. Kelly had seemed a bit jumpy, perhaps a bit more than someone receiving unexpected company. Her uncle and grandfather were covered in varying degrees of mud. Dirt that resembled two men coming in from a hard day on the ranch more than a suburban backyard. "Yes, I do think I want to hear what Miss Edna has to say."

Following behind DJ, Ian tossed the puzzle pieces around in the back of his mind. Absolutely nothing made any sense. He wanted to believe Mrs. Perkins was a senile old woman with a vivid imagination. Twenty minutes later his cop instinct told him this woman had seen exactly what she said. A golf cart disappearing into the thatch behind her house with a cow in tow. What she wasn't sure of was if there had been only one or two people in the cart. It had been a good distance from her home, but close enough for her to be sure of at least the cart and a cow.

Because all of this involved Kelly and her grandfather, Ian refrained from saying anything to DJ about the thoughts and possibilities, or improbabilities, kicking around in his mind. Mostly because he didn't want to believe that Kelly and her family could have anything to do with cattle rustling. They were good people. A family that he and his relatives had known most of their lives. Not cattle rustlers. Not thieves. Her dad had been a beloved high school coach. A sacred position in Texas. There had to be another explanation. Except with every block he passed, moving closer to Kelly's house, all he hoped and prayed for was to find a lawnmower parked in the garage. Anything else would be a nightmare.

Parking just past her house, Ian took his time coming down the sidewalk, slowing at the sound of voices drifting down the drive from the garage. As a friend of the family, he had every reason to be on private property in search of Kelly. As a law officer, he had every reason to believe this could be following a lead. He much preferred the first reason. Slowly he made his way up the drive, the voices coming in louder and the conversation more clearly. Finally close enough to hear the distress in Kelly's voice, Ian realized both he and Kelly were putting very ugly pieces of the truth together. Sucking in a deep breath, he had a decision to make, and fast. Step into the doorway and make his presence as an officer of the law known, or turn and walk away.

• • • •

"Pops." Kelly couldn't believe a word she was hearing. Not that she didn't believe her grandfather was telling her the truth, she just couldn't believe this was really happening. Her sweet, loving, and clearly addled grandfather was stealing cows. "Let me see if I am following this correctly." She enunciated very carefully, not so much for her grandfather to understand, but mostly trying to make herself understand. "You wanted to save the cows?"

Her grandfather smiled. "See. Now you understand."

"No, Pops, I don't." She raised her arms, dropped them again, opened her mouth, closed her mouth, blew out a breath, sucked in more air, all searching for the right words. "I know you don't eat meat anymore. You saw some movie about our food and the treatment of animals, and you made a choice to stop eating animal products. Even though we have been born and raised in the middle of cattle ranching country, I understood that part."

"What else is there to understand?" Her grandfather looked at her with the sense of a young child explaining his perception of the imperfect world.

"What I don't get is how taking," she paused doing math in

her head, "how many cows now?"

"Let's see." Her grandfather and Uncle Ralph looked to the heaven as though counting cattle in the sky. "We didn't want to hit any one rancher too hard."

"And," her uncle added, "we needed to figure out where to keep the cows."

"The abandoned golf course?" Kelly put in.

Her uncle grinned, clearly proud of her understanding. "That's right. Plenty of grass for them to feed on, and some straw spread out in the abandoned clubhouse was perfect for any of the cattle we needed to keep indoors. But we still had to figure out where to send the cows to save them from slaughter."

"And that's where we've run into a little bit of trouble. There doesn't seem to be a whole lot of cattle sanctuaries anywhere. Everybody wants to save retired circus elephants, old zoo cats, or animals illegally smuggled into the country, but not so much cows."

Kelly had no idea what to say. Of course there weren't cow sanctuaries. They were considered a food staple of the United States, not exotic animals. Short of a calf or two at a petting zoo, there was no entertainment value in cattle. Even at state fairs, except for the few stud bulls, the end results for most of the cattle was going to be the meat market. "Pops." She tried not to sound too desperate. "How. Many. Cows. Are we talking?"

"Twenty?"

Uncle Ralph shook his head. "I think we're up to twenty-two, maybe twenty-three."

"Somewhere in there." Her grandfather nodded.

Twenty-two cows. Maybe twenty-three? Kelly might just be sick. With the kitchen door still open, even from where they stood in the garage she could hear the doorbell sound. Company was not what she needed. Plastering on the closest thing to a calm and cool demeanor that she could manage, she waved an arm from her Pops to the cow. "Let's close all the doors before someone sees this guy. We've got to call Adam and DJ, tell them everything—and I mean everything—as soon as I get rid of whoever is at the front door."

Neither old man dared say a word. Her grandfather briefly flashed a scowl, and for a second she thought she saw his lips pucker and mouth open prepared to argue, but instead he nodded, and closing the doors behind them, followed her into the house.

Through the small section of glass, she could make out Ian's features. The sight of him on the other side of the door had her heart doing a fast two step, instantly lifting her mood, until she realized she'd have to explain all of this mess to him as well. If she'd thought her grandfather almost burning down the retirement home and then her own house had been a miserable mess, both incidents were a walk in the park compared to this new disaster. Stealing cattle was a criminal offense that could send her grandfather to jail for whatever time was left of his natural life.

Ian's finger was perched high, ready to ring the bell again when she swung the door open.

"Hellp." She did her best to put on a brave face and smiled as she waved him inside, but the memory of a few hours in jail and the thought of her grandfather spending any time at all behind bars had her almost bursting into tears.

"Hey." He stepped into the house and stopped only a few inches in front of her. "What's the sad face?"

Closing her eyes, she sucked in a deep breath, willing the threatening tears away. "It's such a mess, Ian. Pops is in so much trouble."

Strong hands weaved around her waist, pulling her against him. "Why don't you tell me what's going on?"

Instinctively, she curled into his shoulder. Closing her eyes, refusing to cry, instead feeding on his strength. There had to be a way to make this right, and if anyone would have answers for her, Ian would. She had to trust him. Knew she could trust him. "It's a mess."

Gently stroking her back in slow soothing swirls, his voice rumbled against her ear. "How about starting at the beginning?"

With a nod, she reluctantly slipped out of the safety of his arms, but needing the connection, she kept her fingers loosely entwined with his. She moved to the sofa, sat beside him, and did her best to explain as her grandfather and uncle shifted in their seats like boys called to the principal's office. The words tumbling out like water from a downhill spring, she laid out everything she did and didn't understand. Occasionally her grandfather or uncle added a word here or there, sometimes helping, other times only adding to the confusion. Ian listened patiently, occasionally urging her on with a squeeze of her hand.

The entire convoluted story told, Kelly kept a hopeful gaze on Ian. "Please tell me there's a way out of this mess?"

Ian's shoulders stiffened ever so slightly, but it was enough for her to know he wasn't going to have any easy answers. "One step at a time. We'll need to call both Adam and DJ, but first I'd like you to take me to where you're keeping the cattle." He gave her hand another squeeze. "And if we're lucky, between here and there I'll come up with a brilliant plan."

Despite the wary glare her grandfather shot in her direction, Kelly nodded. At this point she didn't care about brilliant; all she wanted was a plan.

CHAPTER SEVENTEEN

Even though he'd been hoping and praying, not until he'd rung the bell at Kelly's did Ian realize just how badly he'd wanted to find a riding mower in the garage. He also didn't realize how badly he wanted to be an ordinary citizen instead of a law officer until Kelly leaned into him, all broken up over the dilemma at hand. He had no idea how to save her grandfather.

Sure, he knew that his uncle Sean would not press charges against such an old man, especially one who was clearly not functioning out of malice but from an addled older mind. There was definitely another rancher or two that Ian knew would stand with his uncle and not press charges, but he hadn't a clue how the rest of the ranchers would feel about the situation. He could only hope that returning the cattle would be a possible first step to coming out of this mess as unharmed as possible.

"We better start with Uncle Sean. We're going to need to identify the cattle and see what we can do about returning them to their rightful owners."

Kelly's face lit up. "Maybe if we give them back we don't have to make this a police matter?"

"I'm sorry." Ian shook his head. "I have no choice. I have to bring DJ into this. It's his town and I've sworn an oath." The light in her eyes dimmed and he held up his hand. "But that doesn't mean we can't do a little negotiating."

It took only a few minutes to load everyone into his truck and head out to the old golf course. It actually surprised him that nobody around town had noticed the trim lawns of late. Pulling into the parking lot near the old club building, he scanned the distance looking for young cows. Doors slammed, boot heels hit the ground, and circling the hood of the truck, Ian looked to

Kelly's grandfather. "You've done a good job of hiding over twenty cows."

"Maybe." Kelly's grandfather scowled and stomped off around to the back of the building, before spinning around and facing his brother. "You move them inside?"

Uncle Ralph stared slack jaw at the empty greens, shaking his head. "Didn't you?"

Nothing about this conversation made Ian happy. "Are you two saying you've lost the cows?"

"Maybe they just wandered off?" Kelly offered.

Shaking his head, the creases on her grandfather's forehead deepened. "Most of this property either has electric fences or cattle walks so stray cattle and other critters wouldn't wander in and ruin the grounds. We just turned the system on and used it to keep them from wandering out."

"Lord I need a smoke." Uncle Ralph rolled his eyes heavenward.

Kelly's grandfather waved a finger at his brother. "Don't you get me started on that. You know what those—"

"Pops!" Kelly interrupted the two men before they could start a war on the pros and cons of cigarettes. "Where are the cows?"

Staring daggers at his brother, Kelly's grandpa shook his head.

This was so not looking good. "Gentlemen," Ian asked, "you mean to tell me that you don't know where the cows have gone?"

"Oh, I know all right." Kelly's grandpa spun around and stormed off toward the front of the building. "It's that Buford."

Uncle Ralph lit up and snapped his fingers. "Of course."

"Of course what?" Ian lengthened his stride to catch up to the older men. "And who is Buford?"

"That no good, skinny, lazy, scheming Beaumont. He and his brothers never earned an honest dollar in their lives."

Ian had never heard of the Beaumont family. Turning to Kelly, he looked for answers.

Apparently they'd gotten good at reading each other, since

she quickly answered his silent question. "Beaumonts live just over the line in the next county. You rarely run into them. None of the boys went to school. The principal and the teachers all tried to talk some sense into their parents, but neither had any education and didn't see the need for their sons to have it. They live in a piecemeal cabin that's been in the family for generations. No one has ever been sure how they make their living."

"Sure we do," her grandpa insisted. "They're thieving scoundrels."

Ian turned to Pops. "Do you have any reason other than 'they are thieving scoundrels' to think they have your cows?"

The old man slowed by the truck, turning to nod at Ian. "Other day I saw Buford puffing away like a damn chimney just on the other side of the fork in the road to town. Standing around, watching nothing. Said he was waiting on a ride from his brother. Ralph and I drove off and I saw two of those big trucks pull over and he got into one. Wondered where'd they get the money to buy not one but two of those rigs."

Ian was beginning to think he might have the answer to that. "Tell me," he asked Uncle Ralph, "did you do a lot of smoking while watching the Farraday herd?"

"I rarely get to sneak in a cigarette with Mr. Save The Environment around. Besides, we never spent much time watching any of the herds."

"One more question. Did you loosen the fence wires at the Farraday's?"

Both Uncle Ralph and Kelly's grandfather moved their heads from side to side.

Alarm bells rang at full volume in Ian's head. Puzzle pieces were coming together and fast. On the short ride from Kelly's to the club he'd reached out to his uncle who was most likely already on his way to transport the now non-existent cattle. Whipping out his phone, he swiped at the screen, reaching out first to his cousin.

"Didn't expect to hear from you so soon. Need some dating advice?" DJ teased.

"No time to remind you I'm the one who told you to open your eyes about your wife. We have a bigger problem brewing. Did you get the name of the guy they picked up the next county over?"

"As a matter of fact, his prints just came back—"

"A Beaumont?"

"Yeah. How'd you know?"

"Buford is a chain smoker. I think he's the one who was stalking your pastures."

"Shit," DJ mumbled.

"Yeah. And I'm betting any amount of money they just made off with the stash of cattle here at the golf course—"

"What?"

"You heard me. The cattle here are gone. All of them. And I'm willing to bet my badge it's the Beaumonts behind it. If they're moving two trucks of cattle they've got room for a lot more than twenty calves and the next closest ranch to the golf course is—"

"Ours," DJ mumbled.

"Exactly. How much do you want to bet that means—"

"We're next." DJ sighed. "I'll call Dad now. You'll get there before me. Don't do anything stupid."

Ian almost laughed. Talk about the pot calling the kettle black when it came to taking risks to make a collar, DJ was right there with the most brazen of them. "The one you need to tell that to is—"

"Aunt Eileen," they both echoed.

● ● ● ●

"If you ask me, Ian looked way too eager to go all the way to town just for a good deed." Catherine Farraday looked up from helping her daughter with an animal puzzle.

Eileen continued to separate out the flat end pieces. "That's what I said. Adam, Brooks and DJ would all have gladly taken Kelly the leftovers on their way home."

Rocking Brittany to sleep, Allison looked over Aunt Eileen's shoulder and pointed to a flat edge she'd missed. "It's the dog thing."

"You mean puppy thing," Catherine chuckled.

"Puppy, dog, whatever. I've never been a superstitious person, but I'm telling you there's something about these dogs showing up that is totally worthy of a Twilight Zone episode."

"What I want to know is if Kelly was as happy to see Ian as he was to go see her." Eileen handed Stacey another edge piece for her and her mom to link together. Eileen just loved having small children around the house again. She would miss having little Brittany nearby once Ethan and Allison's house was built over near the new hospital. Not that she expected that to happen any time soon with all the construction trouble they'd run into. A few times Sean had come within inches of calling his cousin Patrick to see if he could send a crew in from Oklahoma, but each time the local crew had gotten their act together until the next screw up.

"Do you think this means Ian will transfer someplace closer to Tuckers Bluff or are we going to lose Kelly?" Catherine asked.

Eileen straightened, she hadn't thought about that. Honestly today was the first time since the drive back from Dallas that she'd given any serious consideration to Ian and Kelly as a permanent relationship. A thought she'd actually discarded when she hadn't seen a dog around anywhere that day. Of course what she had yet to figure out at all was how had those two wound up driving together in the first place. Not that it mattered, fate, and the dogs, had an interesting way of turning everyone's lives around.

The old phone on the wall rang. That didn't happen very often. Usually everyone communicated via cell phones.

Pushing away from the table, Eileen reached for the avocado green phone. "Hello."

"Your cell is going straight to voicemail," Sean said.

"I forgot. It's on the charger upstairs."

"We've got a situation. Connor and I are coming back to the ranch. DJ and Ian are meeting us. Ian thinks the cattle thieves could be coming back to the section with the weak fence line.”

“What do you need me to do?”

“Keep the girls in the house. Don’t let Catherine and Brittany go home until we say the coast is clear. He could be wrong and the pasture is nowhere near the house, but I’m not taking any chances with my own.”

“I’ll take care of everyone on this end. You be careful.” The only other crack shot in the family at home now besides her was Hannah. She didn’t know what was happening in the universe but she was getting pretty tired of reaching for her rifle.

CHAPTER EIGHTEEN

"Can't you drive any faster?" If Kelly's grandfather leaned any more forward he'd be sitting on the dashboard.

"Pops, Ian knows what he's doing. Do you want him to stop and set you out at the side of the road?"

What Ian would have preferred was to have left them all behind, but he knew darn well from the way her grandfather was carrying on that two minutes after Ian had pulled out of the driveway the old man and his brother would have been racing after Buford Beaumont on their own. Which meant Kelly would be trailing her grandfather. This way he could at least keep them out of trouble.

The old man harrumphed and sat back in the seat. Kelly and her uncle remained quiet in the back row of the quad cab pick up. The way Ian figured it, DJ was only about twenty minutes behind him coming from the other side of town, and his Uncle Sean should be reaching the ranch just ahead of him. Enough time for Ian to drop his passengers off at the main house with Aunt Eileen, and for Uncle Sean to dump the trailer and saddle a couple of horses for everyone.

Sneaking up on thieves was much easier on horseback. As tempting as it was to go blazing in on four wheelers with sirens, a silent approach was his friend.

"There!" Kelly's grandfather shouted, waving a crooked finger at the road ahead of them. "That's one of them trucks we saw the Beaumonts driving."

Ian slowed and scanned the distance for the second vehicle. A cloud of dust along the back trail told him his gut had been right. Unable to turn off or turn back, he had no choice but to drive past the truck. "Everybody duck down low and stay down till I tell you to come up."

"What for?" Pop spun around to glare at him, but the look Ian shot him was enough to have the old man act now and think later.

The last thing Ian wanted was for anyone in the big rig to recognize all the passengers and grow suspicious. At least if he was the lone driver heading home from town, simply driving by might not raise any red flags. "We're going to drive past the truck, nice and casual, like any other Sunday afternoon."

He couldn't see Kelly and her uncle, but her grandfather grumbled from low in the seat.

Using the bluetooth on his phone Ian called DJ. "What's your ETA?"

"Another thirty to the ranch. Where are you?"

"At the turn off to the South trail. One target is parked at the mouth of the road, the other is heading up the trail."

"Damn it. That's a little closer but you're still looking at twenty till I'm there."

"I'm driving past now." Ian casually checked out the cab. Nothing. "No one in the driver seat. They must have all gone to load the cattle."

Kelly's grandfather popped up from his spot. "Then there's no reason for me to be hiding like a scared rabbit."

"Everyone go ahead and get up," Ian instructed his passengers before returning to his call with DJ. "With no idea how many there are, if they're armed, or how well they're armed, we'll need some backup."

"According to the last rancher they hit, they've got some serious fire power. Don't do a damn thing until Reed or I get there."

"What about your dad?"

"I'll call him and let him know what's going on. I hate to say it, but he can probably get to you faster than we can."

"Got it." Ian cut off the call and debated what the hell to do next with a car load of civilians. Ornery ones at that.

"Now what?" Kelly's voice came out in a near whisper.

Didn't he wish he knew. He had to find out what they were up against and there was only one way to do that. "Here's the plan." He pointed to the two old men. "I don't want the load of cows on the road going anywhere. We're going to check if the truck is unlocked. If it is, you two lock yourselves in the cab until DJ and backup arrive. If there's any sign of the rustlers coming back, and only if they come back before DJ gets here, you turn on the truck and drive it away. Can you do that?"

Chests puffed like peacocks, both men nodded.

"Kelly, you stay here in the pickup. First sign of trouble, call DJ and tell him what's going on." Ian grabbed the rifle from behind the seat.

Kelly's hand landed on his arm. "Promise me you'll be careful?"

The feel of her fingertips against his skin had him stopping short. Without thinking he leaned in and kissed her hard and fast. "Back at you." He had a job to do, but as soon as those idiots were in custody, he was going to sit down and have a long talk with Miss Morgan—and an even longer kiss.

Hurrying away to the foot of the trail, he didn't dare look back over his shoulder. There wasn't a blessed thing about leaving the three of them watching out that he liked. What he would much rather have had was time to drop Kelly and her family off at the ranch where they'd be safe, and DJ a hell of a lot closer to closing in on the rustlers, but as his mother often told them, if wishes were horses, beggars would ride. Hopping over the fence, he scanned the area once again. Keeping eyes forward, he walked low to the ground, made his way quickly up the pasture. Ducking whenever possible behind a grazing cow, he was thankful the truck hadn't gone too far up the dirt trail before stopping to assemble the portable railings to substitute for a pen and chute to load the cattle. From where he stood he counted three men but no sign of the fire power DJ mentioned.

After only a few minutes of watching the Beaumont brothers

trip over each other, struggling to move the full-grown cattle through the makeshift pen and up onto the truck, Ian wondered how the heck they'd managed to get a truckload of cattle from the last ranch they'd hit. Since he wasn't thrilled at the idea of having left the old men in the first truck or Kelly in the pick up, he also considered making his way back to the main road, convinced there was no way they'd be done loading before DJ arrived with backup.

When one of the Beaumonts slipped in a pile of cow dung and landed on his butt, Ian's decision made, he turned to make his way back to the main road, except the truckload of cattle he'd left the old men guarding was now bouncing up the south trail, headlights on, coming at the rustlers full speed ahead, and kicking up dust. Following a car-length behind them; Kelly and his pick up. *Crap.*

• • • •

One lousy minute. Standing by the pick up for a better view of Ian's progress, Kelly had turned her back on her grandfather and uncle to look around for any other signs of life or trouble when she heard the big truck's engine roar to life. *Those stubborn old coots.* Opening the door and scrambling inside the cab of the pick up as fast as she could, she turned the ignition, said a silent prayer to anyone listening, and burned rubber pulling away from the side of the road.

She had no earthly idea what she was going to do when she caught up with her grandfather, but wring his neck was leading the options. Blast that man. And those poor cows bouncing around on a dirt road while her grandfather rode in like a modern day Senior Citizen Lone Ranger. And Tonto too.

The mere size of the truck in front of her and the dust from the tires made it almost impossible to see what was happening ahead. She heard the single crack of gunfire and for the first time since hopping in the cab, realized exactly how dangerous this whole cattle rustling mess really was.

In front of her the large truck came to a screeching halt.

Another shot fired and her heart nearly stopped. The driver's door in front of her burst open and her grandfather flew out waving a huge gun and screaming something that sounded like, "Be careful with the cows, you clods."

"Oh, Pops," she muttered softly, took in a deep breath and ducking low, pushed her door open. "Pops, get back in the truck!"

Somewhere in the recesses of her mind, Ian's words repeated in slow motion—*first sign of trouble, call DJ*. She was pretty sure gunfire counted as trouble. Hitting 9-1-1 on her phone, she didn't wait for Esther to answer before crawling out of the truck for a better look and eased her way around the door that had been keeping her safe. Hiding behind the back end of the cow-filled truck, she heard Esther's voice from her hand.

"What's your emergency?"

"Esther, it's Kelly," she whispered just as another shot fired. "Tell DJ that Ian's in trouble."

"He's almost there. Are you somewhere safe?"

She looked up at the metal truck blocking her view of the people she cared about most in the world and figured the only safer ones were the cows. "I'm fine but tell DJ to hurry."

Slipping her phone into her back pocket, she craned her neck to get a glimpse of what was going on.

• • • •

If Ian could strangle Herbert and Ralph with his bare hands he would. Instead of an easy take down once DJ and Reed arrived, now the doofus brothers had abandoned the cattle and taken up the fire power DJ had warned him of. The only bright side being that they appeared to be as bad a shot as they were cattlemen.

So far, Kelly's grandfather had shot the hat off of one brother and a cattle prod away from another. Whether that was dumb luck or clean shooting, Ian couldn't tell. With Pops threatening to tan the Beaumonts hide if a single cow got hurt, and the three brothers tripping over each other trying to duck Herbert and Ralph's shooting to get away with the few cows they'd managed to load, no one had noticed him circling around with his weapon drawn.

Somewhere behind him a twig snapped and he froze in place, hoping that escaping critters of the four legged variety had made the noise.

The familiar click of a revolver engaging announced the presence of a fourth brother. "I wouldn't take another step if I were you."

Another gunshot sounded and a second brother lost his hat. "Damn it, that was my best hat!" the scrawny man cried.

"I suggest you put your rifle on the ground and tell that crazy friend of yours to do the same, then back away from the truck." Sirens blared in the distance, another crackle of dry brush mixed with kindling sounded behind him, and the hard steel of a gun barrel stabbed into his back. "Now."

"Pops," Ian called out as instructed, his Arms spread wide, he crouched low to the ground, gently setting the rifle down. "I need you to set your weapon on the ground."

"Fat chance," Pops yelled back without looking in his direction.

"I'd listen to him old man" The man sneered with an evil delight. "Unless you want me to put a bullet in his hea..." The words trailed off as a black flash came crashing down hard on the brother's arm, knocking the gun away.

Before Ian could fully process what had gone down, he reached to his ankle holster, and gun in hand, spun around to face his captor only to find the brother writhing on the ground holding a limp arm.

"He made me so mad." Standing over the prone body holding a tire iron, Kelly looked to Ian. "Does it make me a terrible person to hope it's broken? Badly broken?"

Ian held back a laugh and shook his head. "No. Just human." Keeping the gun trained on the fourth brother, with his free hand Ian waved for Kelly to move behind him. "Please come stand over here, and then remind me never to piss you off."

Tossing the tire iron far from the action, Kelly rushed to Ian's side.

Carefully hooking his hand around her waist, he nudged her safely behind him. Across the way muffled voices drew his attention. From the corner of his eye he saw the remaining three brothers lower their weapons.

The blaring sirens as DJ took the corner and barreled up the road overpowered all other sounds, but Ian could see the brothers raising their hands high in the sky. It took another few seconds as the sirens came to an abrupt silence and DJ and Reed bolted out of their police cars for Ian to realize Sean and Connor had crept up from the opposite side and taken the three brothers by surprise.

While Reed ran, gun drawn, to deal with the men Uncle Sean held at gunpoint, DJ came his way. "I'll take it from here. You two go corral the senior citizens I didn't see waving loaded guns around."

Ian nodded and turned to face Kelly. Brushing the back of his knuckle down her cheek, he refrained from pulling her into a bone crushing hug and checking her over from top to bottom to make sure there wasn't a scratch on her. He knew if he took the time to say even one word, DJ would be corralling the old men on his own and Ian would be whisking Kelly away someplace safe, special, and for only the two of them for a very long time. As in for all time. As in wasn't this a crazy damn way to fall in love?

CHAPTER NINETEEN

The living room had been the center of many a Farraday problem solving session. Through the years Kelly had been in awe of the few times she'd watched the family come together and bolster one another through a potential crisis. What she'd never expected was to one day find her own family at the center of such a session.

Even more surprising was sitting on the comfortably aged leather sofa at Ian Farraday's side, their fingers entwined, his thumb gently drawing soothing circles across the back of her hand. Being with him, like this, was the sort of connection she and every girl had dreamed of, though she could have done without the nightmare of people shooting at them a short while ago.

By the time all the dust had settled, the thieves had been taken into custody, her grandfather and uncle had been driven home, most of the Farraday clan had driven out to the ranch for moral support, and Kelly no longer felt the weight of the world on her shoulders. Though that most likely had more to do with the way Ian Farraday looked at her than the rest of the family sitting around the room.

"Then the only problem is our missing calf?" Aunt Eileen asked.

"You mean the *sick* calf at the clinic?" Becky's words weren't meant as a question. The family had drawn together to protect their own. For most of her life Kelly had felt more like family than friend when around the Farradays, but never more than tonight.

"That's right." Adam nodded. "Brooks brought him in earlier today. I don't anticipate any problems there, it's only a cold. He'll be back among the herd pretty soon."

The way everyone managed to tell the absolute truth, with a

totally casual expression, and never mention her garage or her grandfather's antics, was nothing short of amazing. The whole thing almost had Kelly in tears. Only the occasional squeeze by Ian whenever she thought she might lose it kept her from blubbering like a grateful baby.

"It's really quite simple." Sean Farraday leaned forward. "We caught the Beaumonts red handed stealing our cattle. DJ and Reed made the arrests. During this arrest another truck, also registered in the Beaumont's name, was discovered carrying all of the cattle reported as stolen over the last few months. As for my nephew Ian, he's here for a personal vacation. *Only*." Mr. Farraday sat back again. "Seems pretty cut and dry to me."

Catherine nodded. "As an attorney, I'd agree that pretty much sums it up."

"Now the only challenge seems to be how to keep Herbert and Ralph out of any…" Mr. Farraday paused searching for the right word, "mischief."

Aunt Eileen leaned across the side table and patted Kelly's knee. "Don't you worry yourself. We'll figure this one out too. I have a feeling it may be as simple as letting Ruth Ann keep Ralph busy, then maybe on his own Herbert won't be such a handful."

Brother, did Kelly hope Ian's aunt was right.

"All right." Aunt Eileen stood up. "Time for a late night dessert."

"Not for me," Sean said. "Monday morning will be here bright and very early. I need my beauty sleep."

A few voices chorused agreement with Aunt Eileen, a few others echoed the family patriarch's. As the remaining family members mulled about the kitchen, Ian gave her hand a gentle tug and tipped his head toward the back door.

The moon lit the back porch. She loved the peace and quiet that came with a late night breeze on the porch.

"Walk with me?" he asked.

Rather than answer to the moon and back, she settled for a slow nod and a smile.

Hand in hand they followed the narrow path from the house to the barn. Instead of going inside as she would have expected after coming this far, Ian nudged her toward an even narrower path. Only a few feet more, they sat at an old park bench nestled under one of the few mature trees on the ranch.

"This is one of my favorite spots here at the ranch. When I'd visit in the summertime, I'd sit out here with Aunt Helen and she'd tell me stories about the sun, the stars, and the little man on the moon."

Kelly chuckled. She'd never met Mrs. Farraday, but from all the stories the family told, she'd grown to love and miss her a long time ago. "I'm not sure I'd heard the man on the moon story. The immortality of the crab, yes, man on the moon, no."

"Maybe some day I'll share it with you, but right now I'd like to talk about something else."

She was glad he hadn't said anything that required more than a nod, because her mouth had just gone completely dry.

"First, before I say anything more, or worse, something stupid, may I kiss you?"

Surprised by the question, she nodded.

"Really kiss you? I mean, not a nice-to-see-an-old-friend-on-the-cheek kiss, but a man who has been dying to hold you close kind of kiss."

She bobbed her head again and wished he'd just hurry up and kiss her before she did something stupid like throw up on his shoes.

One hand gently cupped the side of her face and the other wound around her shoulder, inching up until his fingers laced through her hair, pulling her closer. So close she could almost feel his heartbeat.

"You're so beautiful," he uttered seconds before his lips came gently down on hers and worshipped her mouth as no man had ever done before.

• • • •

Ian felt like a teenager on a first date with the prom queen. His heart galloped so fast he was sure she could hear every beat. The first touch of her lips on his nearly had him tumbling off balance. The impact, the pressure, the sweetness were almost more than he could take, and yet, would never be enough. Letting his hand slide from the back of her head to rest on her shoulder, he eased away, letting his head fall against her forehead, searching for what to say, wishing they could stay like this forever. "I want more than one kiss."

A sweet smile pulled at the corners of her mouth. "I won't object."

"But I'm going back to work a week from now." He spotted the dejection right away. "If you're willing, I'd like to work around that, at least for a little while."

"Work around?" Her eyes brightened again.

"Days off, that sort of thing, and I don't usually have regular Saturday and Sundays off either, but if I do we can work around that as well."

A hesitant smile appeared. "I can do that."

His finger hooked under her chin, lifting her face level with his. "Will you dance with me?"

"You mean this Friday?"

He shook his head, slipped his phone out from his pocket, swiped at a few apps and set it on the arm of the bench. "I mean now, under the moon and the stars."

Strands of the country version of "Thinking Out Loud" began to play and Kelly melted easily into his arms. He placed a sweet, barely there kiss on her temple, and holding her tight, swayed to the soft notes. He didn't know exactly how they were going to make this work for always and forever, but he knew they would as surely as he knew his name was Ian Brian Farraday.

The song came to an end. Rhythms of the next song blended in with the last and Ian almost felt as well as heard a rustle in the nearby shrubs. He would have gladly ignored it if Kelly hadn't tensed slightly in his arms. "You heard it too?" he asked.

Her head against his shoulder, she nodded. Together they pulled apart and turned in the direction of the movement. He should have known. Sitting quietly like the audience at a famous film festival, the town's two stray dogs sat side by side watching them. When the animals had both his and Kelly's full attention, the one dog lifted her paw up and down and dipped her head as though waving a blessing and giving a nod of approval. Her partner tipped his muzzle upward and gave off one clipped bark.

A smile on her face, Kelly curled back into his arms and without saying a word, continued swaying to the next tune. For a split second his lips tipped up in a smile. Wouldn't his mother be surprised to learn he'd found the right woman behind bars?

EPILOGUE

Not in his entire life had Ian Farraday smiled so much. If Jamie wasn't watching his tough as nails brother with his own eyes, he wouldn't believe it. The man practically glowed. Seeing his brother so darn happy was better than a cold Irish ale on a hot Texas night. Better than Christmas morning for a six year old boy excited to get his first two wheeler. Better than…better than anything—ever.

Every weekend for the last month he'd come to his aunt and uncle's house for a little family time and under the radar recognizance. And much to his surprise, normally busy catching criminals, Ian had managed to appear in town for Sunday supper every week without fail except one. The whole situation had proved fascinating. His normally serious, all-about-the-job brother was tumbling into the home sweet home land of forever after. Damn nice sight too.

Not that Jamie was much different from his brother. He liked women, quite a bit, but bartending wasn't exactly conducive to long term relationships, never mind home and hearth. According to Ian, neither was law enforcement. Though apparently, all it took was the right woman for his brother to sing a different tune.

"Oh my," his mom and Aunt Eileen gushed in choral unison.

Kelly stood in the living room tucked into Ian's side. They'd come back from an early supper in Butler Springs, something Jamie hoped to change in the very near future, and had been chatting for a good fifteen minutes before Kelly moved her hand and the two mother hens squealed with delight.

Little brother moved fast. Based in company C with the Texas Rangers, Ian's home base was only a couple of hours away from the ranch in Tuckers Bluff. Since his vacation and blossoming romance with Kelly, slipping into town on his days off or free weekends had become a common occurrence.

"It's just beautiful." All the women in the family hovered over the ring, shooting questions at the same time, "Have you picked a date? Where are you going to live? You're not leaving us? Are you transferring?" Jamie wasn't sure who said what, but clearly not a soul in the room was disappointed.

"Didn't see that coming." His Uncle Sean stepped in closer, giving the engaged couple more space for hugs and congratulations.

"Really?" When Jamie heard from his mom that Ian and Kelly had shown up for Sunday supper in Austin last weekend, he knew then the sweet gal he'd watched grow up along side his sister and cousin Grace would be his sister-in-law.

Uncle Sean took a short swallow of his after supper glass of milk. The one that came just before the stout. "I knew Kelly was the one, but didn't see an engagement coming this fast."

That hadn't surprised Jamie. When Ian wanted something, he went after it with a vengeance. It was just one thing that made him a good ranger. If Jamie thought about it, just about everyone in the family had that same trait. Determination ran strong in the Farraday DNA.

"Looks like you're the only hold out." Adam slapped an arm around Jamie and tipped his beer bottle at him.

"You make that sound like a bad thing," Jamie teased. He was happy with his life and the new direction coming his way. Some day he wanted what his cousins had one by one found, but there was no hurry. The upcoming pub in Tuckers Bluff was his future, for now.

"Uh oh." Uncle Sean patted Jamie on the back. "Here comes your aunt."

There was no running away from the conversation coming. As Adam had said, he was the last hold out. That whole home, hearth, and fruit of his loins thing was about to be handed to him on a silver platter. Anyone would think with all the weddings and babies surrounding them, his aunt would forget about him.

"Guess this makes you the last Texas Farraday still hanging onto his bachelorhood." Aunt Eileen pushed onto tiptoes and gave her nephew a kiss on one cheek and a pat on the other.

"Looks like it." Last hold out. Check.

"You know, settling down with a good woman has its perks." She turned to Adam. "Doesn't it?"

Home and hearth. Check.

Adam grinned like a fool. "You bet."

All of Jamie's cousins had that sappy grin to them. And they'd all fallen for smart and even somewhat sassy women. No surprise there that they were all happier than pigs in slop.

"And have you ever seen anything as sweet as Stacey playing This Little Piggy with her cousin?"

Fruit of his loins. Check. "Can't say that I have." He smiled at his aunt and pulled her into a big old hug. "I do love you, and I promise you someday I will find that girl and Stacey can play Little Piggy with every one of my fruit."

"Your what?" Aunt Eileen tipped her head back to better see him.

"Children. Sorry. Children."

"Sounds delightful." She tightened her hold around his waist and smiled. "Just don't wait till you're too old to see what's right in front of your face."

No worries there. His eyesight was twenty-twenty and unlike most of his cousins, he wouldn't need any dogs, full grown or puppies, to help him find his soul mate. He chuckled at the thought. After all these years, and a few close calls, it might take something more like a ton of bricks.

MEET CHRIS

USA TODAY Bestselling Author of more than a dozen contemporary novels, including the award winning *Champagne Sisterhood*, Chris Keniston lives in suburban Dallas with her husband, two human children, and two canine children. Though she loves her puppies equally, she admits being especially attached to her German Shepherd rescue. After all, even dogs deserve a happily ever after.

More on Chris and her books can be found at
www.chriskeniston.com

Follow Chris on Facebook at ChrisKenistonAuthor
or on Twitter @ckenistonauthor

Questions? Comments?
I would love to hear from you.
You can reach me at chris@chriskeniston.com